SO-BOA-948

AN INCIDENT
IN ICELAND

AN INCIDENT IN ICELAND

NOAH WEBSTER

PUBLISHED FOR THE CRIME CLUB BY
DOUBLEDAY & COMPANY, INC.
GARDEN CITY, NEW YORK
1979

All of the characters in this book
are fictitious, and any resemblance
to actual persons, living or dead,
is purely coincidental.

Library of Congress Cataloging in Publication Data

Knox, Bill, 1928–
An incident in Iceland.

I. Title.
PZ4.K748Inc   1979   [PR6061.N6]   823'.9'14
ISBN: 0-385-15478-X
Library of Congress Catalog Card Number 79–7513

First Edition

Copyright © 1979 by Bill Knox
All Rights Reserved
Printed in the United States of America

For Edward Robertson
who makes fingerprints.

QUEEN'S AND LORD TREASURER'S REMEMBRANCER

H.M. Exchequer Office.

Para. 30. "by the law of Scotland the Queen's
and Lord Treasurer's Remembrancer is entitled
ex officio to administer without Confirmation
(Letters of Administration) or other process
of law. . . ."

AN INCIDENT
IN ICELAND

CHAPTER ONE

Even the Scottish writer appeared to be showing a suitable respect for the Gleneagles King's Course. The mantle of fresh snow on the Perthshire hills stopped short of its fairways, a pale yellow sun seemed to be trying hard to raise the temperature at least a few degrees, and even the idea that skiing might be the main sport a handful of miles away seemed ridiculous.

Jonathan Gaunt wasn't impressed. Standing on a banking behind the eighteenth green, the grey stone five-star elegance of Gleneagles Hotel nearby, he decided that golf was no game for the reluctant spectator. Sacrilegiously, he wondered how many tons of potatoes the 6,503-yard medal length of fairways might produce if someone had the guts to plough the lot up and start planting.

About a dozen other spectators were scattered around, all watching the two golfers plodding towards the green. Both approach shots had landed adequately close to the pin, bringing muted applause from their audience.

Gaunt shrugged and switched his gaze to the bulky figure beside him. Henry Falconer, senior administrative assistant to the Queen's and Lord Treasurer's Remembrancer, was barely recognisable. Instead of his normal sober business wear he sported a bright blue wool tammy, red corduroy slacks which were too tight for him, and colorful sweater.

Falconer had summoned him north, wrecking his plans for a lazy Sunday morning with a telephone call at an ungodly hour. But when he'd arrived, Falconer had been watching this game—and Falconer seemed determined to see it through.

"One of them should hole for a par five," murmured Falconer suddenly. "They've been level-pegging all the way, so we've got a real finish."

"Amen," said Gaunt bleakly.

He had been in an Edinburgh jazz club till 3 A.M. He had got home to find that the heating in his apartment had broken down again. Then, after Falconer's summons, the drive north had been tricky, with patches of black ice. Now the chill Perthshire air was searing his sinuses and the fortunes of the two players below were among the least of his worries.

A tall, slim redhead caught his attention a few yards away. He had to presume she was slim, because she was swaddled in several layers of sweaters and slacks. Their eyes met briefly and she gave a sympathetic grimace, then the golfers arrived on the green below. One was a visiting American diplomat, the other a middle-league Arab sheik who owned a parcel of oil wells.

As the two men and their caddies began their final rituals, Gaunt glanced again at Falconer. The senior administrative assistant's concentration was on the green.

Gaunt sighed, his freckled, raw-boned face shaping a slight scowl as he stuck his hands into the pockets of his old suede jacket. He'd have to wait—and patience wasn't one of his strong points. Falconer raised that fact regularly as just one of the ways in which he should try harder to blend into the accepted ways of government service, particularly as an external auditor in the Remembrancer's office.

For a start, Jonathan Gaunt didn't look very much like a civil servant: in his early thirties, tall with a compact build, his raw-boned face went with moody grey-green eyes which matched his temperament. Falconer would have added that his fair hair was usually untidy and too long, women called him likeable rather than good-looking, and his taste in clothes leaned heavily towards the casual. By Gleneagles standards his present outfit of wrinkled jacket, tan slacks, grey wool shirt, and scuffed moccasins hardly rated as sporting elegance.

"Now," hissed Falconer.

A moment later he joined the rest of the gallery in a small groan of disappointment as the American missed a putt of a few yards. Stepping forward, his opponent putted in turn and his ball plopped into the cup to win hole and match. A grin touched the corners of Gaunt's mouth as the American sunk his second shot with a casual, expert wrist-flick.

"He threw it, Henry," said Gaunt as the players

dismissed their caddies and headed off towards the club-house. "Diplomacy?"

Falconer nodded. "Probably. We all have to make sacrifices."

They stood where they were for a moment, watching the rest of the gallery disperse. The redhead was among them. She crossed over to join the American, who put an arm round her shoulders.

"I'll buy you a drink," said Falconer.

As an offer, it sounded like a warning bell.

The clubhouse bar was relatively quiet, which seemed to please Falconer. He ordered two Auchentoshan whis-kies, splashed a mist of water into each, paid, then led the way over to an isolated table. He sat silent for a moment, sipping his drink, watching Gaunt do the same.

"All right, let's get started," he said at last. "Tell me something. Have you ever thought of our Queen as a woman?"

"Not particularly." Gaunt raised an eyebrow. "Why?"

"For her age, she's still damned good-looking and has a reasonable figure. Personally, I like her. I can't say I feel the same about her relatives—but who am I to talk with what I've got?"

Gaunt grinned. Henry Falconer made no secret of the fact that he had a wife who scared the hell out of him. A grandfather clock in his Edinburgh office was there sim-ply because Mrs. Falconer wouldn't allow it over the doorstep at home. She said it would clash with the wall-paper.

"Go on," he said. "You're becoming interesting."

Falconer scowled, took a gulp from his glass, and leaned his elbows on the table.

"What I mean is that plenty of people feel the same way. A few of her loyal subjects even leave her something in their wills—tokens of affection in the main. When that happens, it sometimes comes the Department's way and it can be a damned nuisance."

"Hold on." Gaunt was indignant. "Did you drag me up here because some old biddy has left the Royals a china teapot?"

"No. And I thought you'd be glad enough it was nothing to do with golf." Falconer rode the comment with a weary ease. "But a spinster schoolteacher named Violet Douglas died in Aberdeen recently. She left her entire estate to the Queen, though at first that looked as if it would only amount to a few hundred pounds—and the Royals would probably have passed it on to charity." He paused and winced. "Now, suddenly, it's a nightmare. Miss Douglas's estate happens to include a half-share in a highly profitable illegal bootlegging operation."

"For real?" Gaunt gave an incredulous grin.

"Yes, for real," snarled Falconer. He flushed almost as red as his golfing slacks as several heads turned in their direction, and brought his voice down to a hoarse whisper. "About the only thing worse would have been a brothel."

"It isn't," soothed Gaunt. "Where's the location?"

"Iceland."

"It isn't too near home." Gaunt kept the grin on his lips,

but with an effort. Iceland was a place that brought back memories, the kind he could do without. "And the cod wars are over now, Henry."

"But they haven't forgotten them," said Falconer grimly. "If the story gets out that the Queen of Britain has got herself tangled up in liquor smuggling, they'll make the most of it."

"While Thor and Odin fall about laughing?" said Gaunt. As he spoke, he had a feeling he knew at least part of what was coming and didn't like it.

"They're not involved—yet," snapped Falconer, not amused.

"The Douglas woman died about a week ago from natural causes—she was about sixty, but she'd been ill for a spell." He paused long enough to take another swallow of whisky. "Immediately afterwards, word came that her only relative, a younger brother named James, had been killed in Iceland a month earlier—there had been problems tracing his next-of-kin over here."

"You said killed?"

"Accidental death. Some kind of airfield accident, on the ground." Falconer made it plain he wasn't interested. "Douglas had near enough a half-interest in a small air-taxi and freight-hauling company called Arkival Air, which also dabbles in tourist flights—he was a qualified commercial flyer. That's the official side of it, but our Embassy in Reykjavik have some good police contacts and they added the tip that Arkival also happens to be the front for a major bootlegging business that knocks holes through the Icelandic liquor laws."

"Which are tough," said Gaunt. "State-controlled liquor and non-alcoholic beer. It's a good place to go bootlegging."

"Correct." Falconer glanced at him with surprise, then went on. "Anyway, James Douglas was still a British national, loosely domiciled in Scotland. As he didn't leave a will and predeceased his sister she remains his legal heir— or her estate does now, which is where the trouble begins." He sighed and sat back. "The file reached the Remembrancer last night, by special messenger. He phoned my home, my wife told him I was at Gleneagles for a weekend's golf—"

"Living among the fat cats," said Gaunt.

"I'm not in the hotel," said Falconer. "There's a bed-and-breakfast place down the road. Anyway, he contacted me and we agreed our priorities. We need to get someone out to Iceland fast and we need to get shot of Douglas's interests in Arkival Air without anyone suspecting why." He paused. "I don't expect this to brighten your day, but there's a flight out of Glasgow tomorrow. You'll be on it."

It was one of the last things Gaunt wanted. Frowning, he sat back, took out his cigarettes, lit one, and tried for a way out.

"I'm supposed to be helping the Companies Branch team on that off-shore tax fraud—"

"It can wait," said Falconer. "You shouldn't have any trouble in Iceland. They're a highly civilized people, in the main. Admittedly they've got a God-awful language all their own in twelfth-century Germanic or something. But most of them also speak better English than we do."

"What about legal process here? Executors, lawyers, the courts—"

"All arranged." Falconer beamed at him. "Violet Douglas's executor is a respected Scottish solicitor who would love to see his name on the next Honours List. And, of course, the Remembrancer has special powers when the Crown's interests are involved."

"Meaning we can fiddle it," Gaunt said gloomily.

One of the bar windows overlooked the eighteenth. A foursome were struggling in, two in the rough to the right, another thrashing away in a sand-trap bunker before the lollipop-shaped green. He felt rather like the man in the sand-traps—caught and confused.

Falconer was right. When it came to awkward situations, the modern senior-grade professional civil servant who held the medieval Scottish title of Remembrancer usually had an answer available.

In medieval times that was how Remembrancers had survived. Personal bodyservants to the early Scottish kings and queens, charged with literally remembering things for them, they had been a blend of walking notebook and royal conscience. Adapting with the centuries, their web of interest had never stopped growing.

The present Remembrancer operated from a discrete block of offices within the Exchequer Building in Edinburgh's George Street. His total staff consisted of less than seventy men and women, yet as a department they were involved in most government business that mattered in Scotland, whether that meant company law, acting as paymasters, or processing what was vaguely described as "state intelligence." The Remembrancer could even constitute his own court of law, and one of his sidelines was making sure that tax inspectors paid income tax.

Almost anything, in fact, that didn't slot into someone else's regular workload.

"Anything wrong?" Falconer's voice, slightly impatient, cut in on his thoughts.

"No." Gaunt rubbed a hand across his chin. "Nothing that matters. I was day-dreaming."

"You're sure?" Falconer eyed him carefully, frowned, and became more human. "You usually like a chance to escape. If it's—well, if you've a personal problem, say."

Gaunt shook his head. The bulky man opposite, so out of character in his golfing gear, was one of the few people alive who knew him really well . . . though right now there was one thing he didn't know or had forgotten.

"Good." Falconer showed relief. "And I take it the world of stocks and shares hasn't got you by the . . . a—?"

"No more than usual." That was another thing Falconer knew about, that he was the original small-time stock exchange gambler. "I've got some pretty sick tin-mining shares that look like dying, and they're supposed to be my holiday fund."

"Don't cry on my shoulder," said Falconer. "I've got to go back to my wife tonight." He finished his drink and glanced deliberately at his wrist-watch. "A pity you can't stay for lunch. By the time you get back to Edinburgh a messenger should be round at your place with the file, tickets, that sort of thing. The fewer people who know you're in Iceland the better, so don't check with the office tomorrow—I'll say you're on sick leave."

It was dismissal. Gaunt got to his feet.

"You're staying, Henry?" he asked.

"I came here to play golf," said Falconer. "My partner is due any minute—and when you reach my age you occasionally set your own priorities."

"I'll remember," said Gaunt. "We need more people like you."

He left the clubhouse and walked over to the parking lot, where every other car seemed a Rolls-Royce or Bentley. The big names in the pro-am golf world went to St. Andrews, but people who had money chose Gleneagles— and when he reached his own small and dusty Chrysler Alpine, Gaunt had the feeling he should have left it at the tradesman's entrance.

Getting aboard, he started the engine, set the heater grinding, then lit a cigarette and just sat for a moment.

Iceland. He'd been there before all right, briefly enough, but in a way he'd never forget though it was a few years in the past.

Lieutenant Jonathan Gaunt, Parachute Regiment, proud of his red beret and parachute wings, a tiny cog in a NATO airborne exercise, had been flown out with his platoon from Britain to the American base at Keflavik. An hour later they were in the air again, to be dropped into the middle of one of those interior lava deserts the Icelandics called *obyggdir* so that an American team could come and play war games looking for them.

Nice and simple. Till he'd come tumbling out of the sky with a partial chute failure, something still branded in his mind as a screaming nightmare. When the Americans came, it was to airlift him out with a broken back and an ended career.

Gaunt shrugged and took another draw on his cigarette. It had been summer that time, which had meant midnight sun, rain, and black flies. Winter would be— well, maybe the word was "interesting."

He reached for the gear-lever, ready to leave, then left it in neutral as he spotted a small, sky-blue Volkswagen which had just driven in and had parked. The driver was getting out. She was a well-built, cool-looking brunette in her thirties.

Her name was Hannah. She was Henry Falconer's secretary, and she certainly wasn't dressed for work.

A twinkle in his eyes, Gaunt waited until the brunette was safely in the clubhouse before he set the Chrysler moving.

That, at least, was none of his business.

Icelandair operated Boeing 727s on their once-daily five-hundred-mile route from Glasgow to Keflavik and, with a neat advertising touch, called them Saga-Jets. Late in the next afternoon their Monday flight, half-empty because it was the off-season for tourists, eased down through heavy clouds at the end of its ninety-minute flight and met the full fury of a snow blizzard.

At a tourist-class window seat, Jonathan Gaunt listened to the Boeing's hydraulics start a fresh creaking. They were going into a wide, banking circuit and it was easy to see why. Outside, the snow was falling thickly and building against the cabin windows. Down below, tiny pinpricks of moving red light flashed in the early northern darkness as snowploughs worked flat out to get the main runway clear.

He gave a sigh, settled back, saw the NO SMOKING sign was still on, and took the Remembrancer's file from the briefcase on the vacant seat beside him.

The file had been delivered to him by messenger in Edinburgh, as Falconer had promised. With it had come an envelope containing his flight ticket, hotel reservation, and a thick bundle of Icelandic kronur notes plus the usual cautionary note from the cashier's department about expense sheets.

What remained of the Sunday had been too busy for him to do much more than glance at the file. The afternoon had been spent at the weekly poker session run by John Milton, a stockbroker who had to be a friend to tolerate Gaunt's small-time market escapades. The evening had belonged to a brunette who had offered to cook him dinner in her apartment. She was a hospital physiotherapist, cheerfully interested in more than his back muscles, but resigned to the fact that though Gaunt was as healthily normal as any other male there was some reason which left him determined not to become heavily involved.

Even so, the evening hadn't ended the way either of them had intended—and in his own bed that night Gaunt had wakened twice with the sweating nightmare of that drop through space. It had left him dull-eyed the next morning as he packed a bag, left a note for the cleaning woman who looked in twice a week, and finally set off by car for Glasgow Airport.

Deliberately, he pushed that memory out of his mind while the aircraft continued its banking circuit. He'd read through the Remembrancer's file twice already on the flight out but as he flicked through it the parts that mattered registered again.

First, the curtly formal "To Whom It May Concern" letter from the Aberdeen solicitor who was Violet Douglas's executor. Outraged sentiments lay behind the careful wording which declared that Gaunt had full powers to act in all matters concerning the dead woman's affairs without in any way indicating why. That was followed by some photostats of the letters and documentation, most of it involving the Embassy in Reykjavik, which had led to Violet Douglas being traced as her brother's sole relative and heir.

He passed that over in favour of another photostat, the cautious but thorough confidential memorandum which some junior embassy official had fired off as a hopeful end to the affair without any knowledge of the alarm and consternation that would result.

When he died, James Douglas had owned 49 per cent of Arkival Air, which was a small but financially healthy operation. Forty-nine per cent was the maximum interest any foreigner was allowed to hold in any local company under Icelandic law, and the rest of the equity in Arkival belonged to his partner and the firm's managing director Lief Ragnarson. The main assets, apart from offices, hangar space and similar facilities, were two twin-engined six-seater Cessna aircraft, and the embassy official suggested that Arkival's paper valuation was probably in excess of two hundred thousand pounds sterling.

The final paragraph was the one that really mattered.

"Outstanding bank loans may considerably reduce the above figure. But Miss Douglas's executor should be advised that a continued interest in the Arkival company might entail embarrassing consequences. Local police inquiries have for some time suggested that the firm is used as a front for illegal liquor smuggling on a substantial scale. Proof apparently falls short of prosecution, partly because Icelandic liquor law is not popular with a certain section of the population. But Lief Ragnarson, a most forceful individual, is believed to head this activity and it must be assumed that the late James Douglas was also involved."

It ended there, hinting at a wealth left unsaid and the possibility that someone on the embassy staff was a customer sadly choosing between private interest and duty. Grimacing, Gaunt stowed the file away again and went back to that day's copy of the *Financial Times*. He knew the part that mattered there too—his tin-mining shares were just as sick as ever. This time, he worked out exactly how much he'd lost to date, then wished he hadn't.

But there was another piece, the story of why the next International Monetary Fund meeting in Paris had been hurriedly brought forward a few days. Another European financial crisis was shaping. Still, he decided, it was nice to know other people had their own money problems.

The Boeing had to complete two more circuits before the runway below was pronounced cleared. Then the Icelandair pilot didn't waste time. The jet heaved round in a way that brought a last-moment scurry of cabin staff and moments later they were down, racing past a flicker of runway lights through a grey darkness which seemed filled with snow. Still not wasting time, the jet quickly taxied off the runway and came to a halt close to a small, brightly lit terminal building. A squad of hooded, muffled ground staff were waiting and soon the first passengers were disembarking.

Turning up his coat collar as he emerged, Gaunt hurried like the others across the gap between aircraft and terminal building, following a roughly cleared path. The snow was still falling heavily and had drifted to a height of several feet against the terminal's frontage. But warmth met him like a wave inside, his passport was perfunctorily stamped by a plump, bored immigration officer, and he went through to the baggage hall.

Standing beneath an advertising sign, he lit a cigarette and looked again at his fellow passengers. A few were the inevitable tired-faced businessmen found on any flight; a new country, just a different hotel room. Most of the others were obviously Icelanders returning home, already talking busily to the airport staff, catching up on local news and gossip.

But there was something different about three men standing together a little way back from the rest. All in their late twenties and casually dressed, each with a small, orange-coloured flight bag slung over one shoulder, they still didn't fit any tourist category. Two were talking quietly, the third only half-listening while his sharp, bright eyes kept glancing around, alert to anything happening near him.

Then the luggage began arriving and the other passengers closed in. Joining the crowd, Gaunt saw his battered travel bag appear, grabbed it, and headed for the green NOTHING TO DECLARE channel through customs. The three men with the orange flight bags were just ahead of him and the solitary customs officer on duty nodded them through. But he stopped Gaunt.

"Tourist?" he asked cheerfully.

"No, a business trip." Gaunt opened the bag and watched the man make a brief, surface examination. "Or it will be, if I can get to Reykjavik."

"Worried by this little bit of snow? Here, we don't notice it." The man grinned and closed the bag, satisfied. "*Takk . . .* where are you staying?"

"The Loftleider Hotel."

"Then you're in luck. The airline bus will take you right to the door. Enjoy your stay." He waved Gaunt on.

The exit from the terminal was a short distance along a corridor. Stepping out into the darkness again, Gaunt found it was still snowing heavily but the airline coach for Reykjavik was waiting almost at the door. Suddenly a bright red mini-bus parked behind it caught his eye. It had Arkival Air on the sides in large black letters and the last of the three men he'd noticed earlier was getting aboard it.

Acting on impulse, Gaunt turned towards the mini-bus just as its door closed and the engine started up. Headlights blazing, the mini-bus pulled away in a spatter of slush from its tyres, giving him the briefest glimpse of a dark-haired good-looking girl behind the wheel and a rough count of six men aboard as passengers.

Then it had gone and, turning back, he boarded the airline coach. The driver a small, bald man with a cigarette dangling from his lips, nodded a casual greeting.

"Who gets to use the bus from Arkival Air?" asked Gaunt, paying his fare.

"Their own people." The man saw Gaunt wanted more, and shrugged. "They fly from the domestic *flugvoller* at Reykjavik, not from here. So they run their own courtesy service when they've passengers coming in or going out international."

"See them out here often?"

"*Ja*, often enough."

"How do they rate?" persisted Gaunt.

"I mind my own business. They're people who don't take kindly to outsiders who ask questions. Look, is there something about my bus you don't like, *herra?*"

"It'll do," said Gaunt. "But Arkival have a prettier driver."

The man grinned, showing a set of broken teeth, and thumbed Gaunt in towards the nearest vacant seat.

Keflavik—airport, U.S. military base and town—sits on a tongue of land in Iceland's south-west peninsula. From there to Reykjavik, the capital, is a thirty-five-mile journey to the east by road, most of it within sight of the shore-line.

Airline coaches ran to a tight schedule, and from the start the bald-headed driver seemed determined to show that a few inches of snow was a mere incidental. Screen wipers slapping briskly, the coach snarled away from the airport, passed the U. S. Air Force checkpoint, and built up speed as soon as it reached the narrow, busy main highway.

The snow had begun to die away, and soon ended, which helped. They passed a couple of cars which had skidded off and lay slightly crumpled in ditches but the rest was just a procession of headlamps hurrying both ways along a flat, white monotony of road through a darkness. Gaunt closed his eyes and let the distance pass, trying to ignore the familiar discomfort building in his back.

Eventually, when he looked around again, they had reached the outskirts of Reykjavik and were travelling through the suburbs. From appearances, the city had escaped the worst of the blizzard and life was normal. School patrolwomen with lighted batons stopped the coach now and again, shepherding children across the streets at the end of classes, and as the sky cleared the moon shone down on the corrugated iron roofs of rows of neat apartment blocks and bungalows. Veering away from the lights of the city, they skirted the domestic airport perimeter. The Loftleider Hotel was a big, modern building on the far side, only a tall wire mesh fence separating it from a parking apron occupied by a number of light aircraft.

The coach unloaded, Gaunt entered the hotel and checked with the desk clerk. A young porter carried his travel bag along to his room. As the door closed, Gaunt gave a satisfied glance around the spotlessly clean, Scandinavian-style layout, dumped his coat and jacket on a chair, then went over to the window. It was double-glazed for insulation, but looked out across a road and the perimeter fence to the main runway. He watched a medium-sized freighter take off then turned away, found the bottle of pain-killer pills in his bag, swallowed a couple, and flopped down gratefully on the bed. As long as he was moving, everything was fine. It was when he was cramped in one position that the ache still built.

The bedside telephone suddenly rang. Cursing mildly, he rolled over and answered it.

"*Herra* Gaunt?" It was a man's voice, gruff and confident. "Lief Ragnarson—I had a cable from Scotland to say you were arriving. Maybe the sooner we meet the better, eh?"

"You don't waste time." Frowning, surprised, Gaunt sat upright. "All right, where are you?"

"Down below you, in the hotel bar." Ragnarson paused and chuckled. "Look for someone fat and middle-aged—or ask. Most people know me."

Gaunt hung up the receiver, grimaced, and rose. He'd known the cable was being sent by the Remembrancer's office, but he hadn't expected such immediate reaction. James Douglas's surviving partner was obviously keen to find out what was going on—it could be a shade too keen. Straightening his tie, he pulled on his jacket again, then glanced at his reflection in a mirror. The grey Donegal tweed suit he was wearing was crumpled from travel, his faded blue shirt had been chosen for comfort, and the result wasn't impressive. But it would do. Checking that his briefcase was locked, he left it lying and went out.

CHAPTER TWO

The hotel bar was on the ground floor, busy without being crowded. When he got there, Gaunt saw a heavily-built man sitting on his own at a table against a wall, a green parka hanging over the back of his chair. The man grinned at him, nodded, and he crossed over.

"Welcome to Reykjavik." Lief Ragnarson rose to his feet, a guarded smile on his broad face. He was middle-aged, like he'd said, and not much more than medium height. But he was built like a bull from the shoulders down and not too much of it looked like fat. Dressed in a white fisherman-knit sweater and smartly cut grey slacks, he had thinning red hair, brown eyes, and a handshake which held a bone-crushing potential. Pushing out a chair, he waved an invitation. "Sit down. If you're a Scotsman, then like Jamie Douglas you drink whisky. But try our local *brennivin*, okay?"

"Thanks." Gaunt sat down and stayed silent while Ragnarson signalled a waiter over and ordered. Then he asked, "How did you hear I'd arrived?"

"I have a friend in the airline at Keflavik, and I know

the desk clerk here." Ragnarson considered him calmly
for a moment. "*Ja*, I expected someone to come over
eventually to sort out this business, but there is something
I don't understand. I was told Jamie had a sister in Scotland, a woman we hadn't known about. But the cable
about you came from a British government agency.
Why?"

"His sister died before word came through about him."
Gaunt found the follow-up lie came easily enough. "There
are tax problems, legal problems, no other family anyone
can find—her lawyer had to talk to us."

"Tax problems." Ragnarson's eyes hardened. "So, that
makes you some kind of official grave-robber?"

"Grave-robbing is a separate agency," said Gaunt. "I'm
just a helping hand to get things moving. You want that,
don't you?"

Ragnarson hesitated, gave a reluctant nod, and left it at
that as the waiter returned with their drinks. As the man
left, he raised his glass.

"To your visit," he said. Then, as they drank, he
watched Gaunt's reaction with a faint hint of amusement.
"I should have warned you. We have another name for
brennivin—we call it the black death. It is a—well, a distant relation to schnapps."

Gaunt nodded, left speechless, the spirits still burning
down his throat. Unperturbed, Ragnarson took another
swallow of his drink, set down the glass, and took a casual
look around the bar. The mix of customers were domi-
nated by typically lean, fair-haired young men and
women with raw-boned Scandinavian features, travel-

poster models come to life in cheerful, noisy groups. A few caught his glance, grinned, and waved. Ragnarson did little more than nod in return.

"Our smart set," he said caustically, and brought his attention back to Gaunt. For a moment the fingers of one large hand tapped a slow tattoo on the table-top, as if he was thinking. "You say you came here to help out. How?"

"Maybe by giving you first chance to buy your late partner's share in Arkival Air," said Gaunt. "A fair price and no haggling. You make the offer."

"You have that authority?" The big man opposite raised an eyebrow.

"In writing," confirmed Gaunt. "First, I need to know what I'm selling, but after that—"

"*Ja.*" Ragnarson sucked his lips thoughtfully. "And I would need a little time to work things out, to talk to some people—including my wife and my bank. But I'm interested." He paused for a moment, then added, "I have an idea. If you have an hour to spare, get your coat. We can take a trip over to the hangar and office now—it might help."

Gaunt agreed. They left the bar and Ragnarson waited in the hotel lobby while he went up to his room for his coat. When he returned, Ragnarson led the way out into the darkness and they crunched across the crisp snow in the parking lot to Ragnarson's car, an elderly, green two-door Saab. Once aboard, Gaunt saw that the interior showed signs of hard wear, but the engine fired first time and purred sweetly.

"Damn weather," said Ragnarson without rancour, setting the Saab moving. "We had to cancel a couple of flights this morning, and just managed to get a passenger flight off this afternoon, before I came over."

"I saw an Arkival Air mini-bus at Keflavik," said Gaunt.

"Our only mini-bus," corrected Ragnarson. "We're no big airline. It was collecting five students flying out to Alfaburg—the flight I was talking about." He had the car moving along the road which followed the domestic airport boundary from the hotel and swore as a passing truck threw a mixture of snow and slush across the windscreen. "You know about Alfaburg?"

Gaunt shook his head.

"It's a school—a kind of school, anyway. A Swede called Harald Nordur runs it, out in the middle of nowhere—the only sensible way in and out is by air. He has a whole string of big international companies who fly in their junior management from different countries. Then they spend two weeks or so at what he calls initiative testing, which means having their tails chased over a damn lava wilderness like they were so many Boy Scouts. You know the sort of thing?"

"Survive and you get a certificate," said Gaunt. There were similar courses he'd heard about in other countries—big business had been sold the idea that if you hauled a junior executive away from his familiar office environment and dumped him in totally alien surroundings for a spell, the results told a lot. He grinned to himself. In the army, it usually revealed who could run the best poker school. "How many do they take at a time?"

"It varies—ten to twenty, but never more."

As he spoke, Ragnarson slowed the car. They turned off the road and through an opened gate in the boundary fence, tyres crunching on rutted snow as they followed a perimeter track which led past a series of hangars and huts, some brightly lit, others in darkness. The main runway was clear, a broad black ribbon on which an aircraft had just landed while another moved in, ready for take-off.

A grunt from his companion brought Gaunt's attention round again. Just ahead was a large hangar building with a small office block like an extension at one side. Along the front of the office block, lit by a spot-lamp, a large red and black signboard said ARKIVAL AIR. They drew in and stopped beside a handful of other vehicles in a parking lot beside the hangar. Switching off, Ragnarson reached for his door handle.

"Tell me one thing," said Gaunt, stopping him. "Just what did happen to Jamie Douglas?"

"He made a mistake. You see our aerial mast?"

It was above the office block, a slender silhouette rising high into the night and topped with a red warning light. Gaunt nodded.

"That was Jamie's toy." Ragnarson leaned his elbows on the steering wheel, his face grave in the faint light. "It killed him. All we know is he came back here alone that night to finish some work, and he was lying dead the next morning on the roof, at the foot of the mast. There was a break in the aerial wire, he had tools with him to repair it —but the transmitter was still switched on in the office."

Gaunt winced. "Electrocuted?"

Ragnarson nodded. "The transmitter is a powerful one,

with what the experts call an extra high frequency output. With the transmitter left on—" He gave a shrug. "It had been a bad day for weather and he had been flying most of it."

"And when a man gets tired, he gets careless," said Gaunt. "Who found him?"

"I did," said Ragnarson almost curtly. "Now, shall we go in?"

They left the car and Ragnarson led the way to a small service door lying in shadow at one side of the hangar. Opening it, he motioned Gaunt through, then followed, closing the door again behind them.

It was warm and bright inside the hangar. The red mini-bus was parked to one side, a pick-up truck and a couple of other vehicles lay at the rear, and a slim red twin-engined aircraft, a six-seater Cessna, sat in the middle of the main hangar space. A lanky, balding horse-faced man in overalls was working on the starboard engine. Gesturing Gaunt to wait, Ragnarson walked over. The two men talked for a moment, the horse-faced man shaking his head. But finally Ragnarson slapped him on the back and returned.

"Our mechanic, Pete Close—a pessimistic Englishman, though he had the good sense to marry an Icelandic girl," said Ragnarson, guiding Gaunt across the hangar area to another door. "With him, nothing is ever simple. We had a power-loss problem with that engine, from the fuel feed. He has it sorted out, but he likes to moan."

"The right of all engineers," agreed Gaunt. "When will your other aircraft get back?"

"Soon—in an hour or so at most, depending on the turn-

around time at Alfaburg. This snowfall was fairly local so
it shouldn't be delayed." Opening the door, Ragnarson
waved Gaunt through. "Do you know the aviation business?"

"I buy a ticket and hope the man up front knows what
he's doing," said Gaunt as they started down a small corridor.

"Like me, once things get off the ground," admitted
Ragnarson. "*Ja,* and I keep my seat-belt fastened till we
land." He shrugged. "Jamie was different—he shared the
flying with our two regular pilots. They work harder
now."

They emerged in the office block, in a large room which
held a scatter of desks and filing cabinets. The only person in the room, a strikingly large, middle-aged woman,
sat behind one of the desks tapping at a typewriter which
seemed dwarfed by her size. She stopped as she saw them
and rose, smiling at Gaunt, giving a quick, questioning
glance at Ragnarson.

"Now you meet the real boss around here," said Ragnarson proudly. "This is my wife, Anna Jorgensdottir—
and Anna, this is the Jonathan Gaunt we got the cable
about."

Anna Jorgensdottir wore a tailored two-piece blue suit
with a white blouse, was if anything taller than her husband, and was built to match. Her long, blond hair was
greying but she was still a good-looking woman. She also
had a near crushing handshake.

"Call her Anna," suggested Ragnarson. "We mostly use
first names, okay?"

Gaunt nodded. In a country where the telephone directory listed subscribers by their first manes, where women usually kept and used their maiden names after marriage, and where a child's surname was mostly formed by adding *son* or *dottir* to the father's first name, it could only make life easier. Though the maiden name part probably startled hotel clerks when an Icelandic couple went abroad.

"Good." Anna Jorgensdottir turned to her husband. "Have you had a chance to talk yet?"

"*Ja*, enough for now. I'll tell you later. Some coffee, woman—and where is everyone?"

"They're around," she said vaguely, then frowned. "And Harald Nordur is here—he says he has to see you urgently."

"Now?" Ragnarson swore softly, then turned apologetically to Gaunt. "I told you about him. He runs the Alfaburg camp. Where is he, Anna?"

"I put him in Jamie's office." She laid a hand on his arm as he turned to go. "Lief, your Aunt Erna telephoned, to ask if you remembered about tonight."

"Tonight? I thought—" Ragnarson sounded surprised but stopped it there. He pursed his lips and nodded. "*Takk*. Call her back and say we'll be there. I'll find out what Nordur wants."

He went across the room, opened a door which gave a glimpse of a small private office, and went in. As the door closed again, Gaunt heard a man's voice.

"Your first time in Iceland, Mr. Gaunt?" asked Anna Jorgensdottir politely.

"Second—but the first with a chance to look around."
Gaunt rubbed a hand along his chin. "I noticed you said
Jamie's office—Lief must miss him."

"They were friends as well as partners," she said
quietly, then gestured towards a chair. "Sit down—I'll get
you that coffee."

She went off and disappeared into a back room, moving
lightly for her size, while Gaunt sat down. Opposite him,
a large section of wall was filled by a map of Iceland
studded with marker pins. Paperwork was scattered on
the desk, a model of an old biplane hung from the ceiling,
and a radio receiver gave a low hiss of static from a shelf.

Lighting a cigarette, he settled back and drew on the
smoke, letting it out slowly. So far, things appeared to be
going smoothly towards doing a deal with Ragnarson and
the big man seemed likeable enough. If anything, he had
the feeling that Ragnarson and his wife had been nervous
about his visit, but that could be for another reason.

Gaunt smiled to himself. If the Ragnarsons did run a
bootleg liquor operation on the side it stayed none of his
business—and neither gave the impression of being the
type who left loose ends lying around for strangers to trip
over.

His eyes strayed back to the map again, to the vast,
empty stretches which filled most of the interior. A small
air-taxi and freight outfit like Arkival Air could tie in
neatly—as well as make good business sense on its own.
Three-fifths of Iceland was barren, uninhabited volcanic
desert or ice glacier, an off-moment of creation. The rest,
outside of Reykjavik itself and a few smaller towns, was a

fringe of tiny, widely separated settlements, only a minority linked by decent roads. The aeroplane might have been invented for Iceland—or Iceland for the aeroplane.

He left the thought there as Anna bustled back with a tin-lid tray. It held a mug of black coffee flanked by sugar and powdered milk in a pair of screw-top jars. She put it down with a smile, then crossed to the hissing radio receiver and switched it off.

"I have to listen when we have an aircraft flying and there is no-one around in the radio room," she explained. "But the moment they come back, off it goes—before it drives me crazy."

"You work here full-time?" asked Gaunt.

"*Ja.* Lief and I have no family." Her broad face crinkled. "And this way, I can keep an eye on him."

She left him again. Gaunt had stubbed his cigarette and had finished the coffee before the private office door opened. The man Lief Ragnarson ushered out was slim, medium height, and in his early thirties. Harald Nordur didn't match the outdoor notion of an adventure-training school boss—he had a sallow skin, wavy dark hair, and wore metal spectacles. A fur-lined gaberdine coat hung loose over his dark grey business suit, the trouser cuffs tucked neatly into calf-length rubber boots, and his shirt and tie were a colour-matched blue.

The other thing about him was that his eyes had an ill-tempered glitter. As they passed Gaunt, the dark-haired man gave him a curt nod but didn't slow.

The two men went out into the corridor. Gaunt heard the low mutter of their voices for a moment, then a door opened and was banged shut again. Coming back into the room, Ragnarson sat himself on the edge of a desk and thumped a fist hard on the wood.

"Trouble?" asked Gaunt.

"I don't like damn Swedes who walk in and tell me how to run things," snarled Ragnarson, combing a hand through his sparse red hair in an angry gesture. "If he expects me to say *takk fyrirr* and kiss his damn rubber boots, he's wrong."

"But you didn't exactly throw him out," said Gaunt.

"*Nei.* He still wants to spend money. He wants extra flights which will foul up other customers, he wants to choose his pilot, he wants this, he wants that—right. Hell, I'll give him most of what he wants. But not everything, so he knows he doesn't own me. And it's going to cost him till it hurts."

"The sensible approach," agreed Gaunt. "It's called business ethics. Next thing, you'll be invited to join a Rotary Club."

Ragnarson laughed, came down off the desk, and went over to a filing cabinet. Opening it, he fingered through the folders inside for a moment.

"Suppose I give you something to read, and you came back tomorrow, about noon?" he suggested. "This is a rundown on Arkival Air put together after Jamie died, when our lawyer thought we might have tax problems." He stuffed the papers into an envelope and handed them over. "Then—well, this was Jamie."

It was a colour snapshot, taken in summer. Posed beside the cockpit of a light aircraft, James Douglas had been a tall, slim man, still handsome, with black hair streaked with grey and a thin moustache. Standing in slacks and an open-necked shirt, he was giving the camera the full benefit of a sardonic grin.

"How did you meet him?" asked Gaunt, handing back the photograph and tucking the envelope into an inside pocket.

"It was six, seven years ago." Ragnarson frowned at the photograph. "I had seen him around a few times—he was flying for one of our local airlines, bus-run stuff. He had a little money, he wanted to start on his own, but our law said he had to have an Icelandic partner—"

"You weren't in aviation?"

"Me? Hell, no. I was raised to be a fisherman. But Jamie knew flying. He had been a pilot in your Royal Air Force, with a medal from Korea. Afterwards—I think he had made mistakes. But we did well together." He went back, returned the photograph to the filing cabinet, and closed it. "Now, I must sort out these arrangements for that damn Swede. But first"—he raised his voice to a bellow—"Anna!"

Anna Jorgensdottir's formidable figure appeared from the back office area, as if on cue.

"Has Chris gone home yet?" demanded her husband.

"*Nei.*" She shook her head. "You told her to check those freight lists, remember? She's stuck in that cupboard you call a stock room."

"Chris fits in it easier than you do," said Ragnarson without malice. "Ask her to give our friend a lift back to his hotel. And . . . ah . . . did you speak to Aunt Erna?"

"She sends her love till tonight," she nodded.

As his wife went away, he shifted his feet uncomfortably.

"This girl," he said abruptly. "Her name is *Fru* Christine Bennett—she's Icelandic, but she married an Englishman while she was working in London. They came back to Iceland, then they divorced. Now—well, she helps with most things around here."

"So?" Gaunt raised an eyebrow.

"I thought you should know," shrugged Ragnarson. "She had a bad time, that's all. Sometimes she still says crazy things—"

"Like what?"

"Just remember what I said," said Ragnarson. He paused, embarrassed. "Specially if she talks about how Jamie died."

"She was friendly with him?"

"Not the way you mean. They talked sometimes, that's all."

"I'll remember." Gaunt took his chance. "Stories don't worry me too much. I've even heard a few about you."

"*Takk*," said Ragnarson. "Someday I'll maybe write a book about the things I'm supposed to have done. Do I look like a crook?"

"Do the best?" asked Gaunt. He saw Ragnarson give a lopsided grin, then left it at that. A girl was coming towards them from the back office, the same girl he'd seen driving the mini-bus at Keflavik.

She was tall and slim, her hair not dark, as he'd thought, but a fine copper-bronze, long enough to brush the shoulders of the white wool parka she wore over a dark blue sweater and matching slacks. She also had brown eyes, a fine-boned face, and a mouth that looked as though it hadn't completely forgotten how to smile.

"Chris, this is Jonathan Gaunt, your passenger," said Ragnarson. "Deliver him in one piece. Right now, he matters."

She nodded to Gaunt.

"My car's out front," she said crisply. "If you're ready?"

He said good-bye to Ragnarson and followed her out of the building, through another door which led straight into the car park. It had grown colder, and he was glad to get into the passenger seat of her car, a small blue Ford.

"How long have you been with Arkival?" asked Gaunt conversationally as she started the car and set it moving.

"About a year." Her attention stayed firmly ahead as they skirted the hangars. "Why?"

"I'm interested." Gaunt waited until they had passed through the perimeter gate and were back on the road outside the airport. Then he went in deliberately. "Ragnarson says you've some notions about why James Douglas died."

The car swerved as she turned to stare at him. Quickly, the girl flicked the wheel to steady it. He saw her mouth tighten.

"Well?" he waited.

"Lief Ragnarson talks too much," she said. "And you meant 'crazy notions'—that's what he calls them. Anyway, they don't add up to much, just that Jamie seemed worried. I don't know why."

The girl left it at that, her expression discouraging conversation. Soon, the lights of the Loftleider Hotel were on ahead. As the car began to slow, turning in, Gaunt tried again.

"Like to stop off for a drink?" he asked. "I'd like to hear more about what happened."

"There isn't more." She shook her head. "And I've got a date, sorry." Stopping the car at the hotel entrance, she gave him a slight smile. "Anna said you come from Edinburgh. I was there once, when I was small. It was disappointing—I thought all Scotsmen would wear kilts."

"I left mine at home," said Gaunt. "About that drink— as far as I know, you didn't say 'never.' Can I ask another time?"

She looked at him thoughtfully for a moment then nodded. He grinned, got out of the car, closed the door, then watched it drive away before he turned and went into the Loftleider's warmth.

Once in his room, Gaunt spent the next hour checking through the financial breakdown Ragnarson had given him. At the end, he still had a few calculations of his own to make, but the picture was a lot clearer. Arkival Air made enough of a profit to keep healthy, but there was a large bank loan in the background, and several payments were still due on the two Cessna aircraft, which had been bought second-hand to replace an older pair.

And Ragnarson had been right about one thing—the contract with the Alfaburg training centre was one of the best in the company's books. He put the typewritten sheets aside and lit a cigarette. On the figures, the Arkival operation had every chance for growth but it just wasn't happening, as if the partners almost opposed the idea.

He grimaced, remembering the suggested bootlegging operation in the background and Ragnarson's bland denial. Then, though it had no relevance, he recalled what Chris Bennett had said about James Douglas's worried tension before he died.

Gaunt's thoughts drifted to the girl and the way she had looked when she smiled. Divorce meant a rough time for anyone.

It still hurt when he thought of Patty. They'd tried, but she married a set of paratroop wings more than a man. At least she hadn't told him things were wrong till after he was discharged from military hospital—and there hadn't been children.

So they'd divorced, still friends. And she'd remarried, her new husband a likeable character who tried not to act embarrassed when they met.

Leaving Gaunt with his personal nightmare about falling, an army pension, his pain-killer pills, and a total, drifting lack of purpose. A few University terms studying law and accountancy before the army was a pretty nebulous asset in a civilian world . . . until somebody—he still didn't know who—had decided the Remembrancer's Office could use him and had been right.

Everybody started living again, sooner or later. Even if they didn't totally forget. Chris Bennett would find that out eventually—he hoped.

A little later he went along to the hotel restaurant and

picked his way through the menu while he sipped a glass of weak, flat-tasting local beer. It was his first taste of Icelandic food—the American base had been strictly steak-orientated—and he experimented cheerfully with their sheep's-blood bread, made the mistake of trying ripened shark meat which he couldn't even get past his nose, and finally sought refuge in smoked lamb, which made up for all the rest.

He was in no hurry and there was a piano playing. He nursed another glass of beer when he was finished, watched the other guests who came and went, and at last, almost reluctantly, headed back to his room about an hour before midnight.

Gaunt was whistling to himself as he went to put his key in the lock. Then he stopped short as the door moved and opened to his touch.

Tight-lipped, knowing he had locked it, he pushed the door fully open, snapped on the light switch, then swore. His travel bag had been emptied on the bed and its contents thrown about. Beside them, his locked briefcase had been opened by the simple expedient of slashing the leather apart with a knife, and the papers it had contained were scattered around.

Closing the door with his heel, he considered the mess and decided nothing seemed missing. The curtains were open, and he started towards them, still cursing to himself.

Before he got there, the telephone began ringing and he answered it curtly.

"Mr. Gaunt?" The voice in his ear was male, relaxed,

and yet commanding attention. "We saw your light come on. I'm afraid we owe you an apology."

"For what?" Gaunt's anger came boiling. "If you mean you're the character who—"

"Who was in your room, yes. At least, I was responsible." The man at the other end sounded almost amused. His English held a faint background accent that was difficult to place. "Call it an error of judgement, a mistake I'd like you to forget."

"Like hell I will," snapped Gaunt.

"Look inside your briefcase," suggested the voice. "Consider what's there as compensation."

Puzzled, Gaunt reached for the briefcase, shook it, and stared at the wad of kronur banknotes which tumbled onto the bed.

"I see it," he said grimly. "Go on."

"Compensation," repeated the voice in his ear. "A hotel pass-key was . . . ah . . . borrowed and returned, so we have no problem there. All you have to do, Mr. Gaunt, is be sensible and forget."

"It would help if I knew why," said Gaunt.

"When someone who works for the British Government comes to visit Lief Ragnarson, we want to know if he matters," said the man at the other end of the line, his voice hardening. "Now we know you don't, and my people wish no trouble. So you have the chance to finish your business, keep quiet, and forget any notion about complaining to the police—or Ragnarson."

"Supposing I don't?" demanded Gaunt.

"Go over to your window—the phone will reach," came

the curt instruction. "Look down—tell me if you see a snowman that the children have built."

Gaunt went over, knowing he constituted a target in the lighted window, taking the chance. He looked down, and saw the snowman beside the airport perimeter fence.

"I see it," he said.

"And the three bottles on its head?"

He looked again, and saw the glass bottles glinting in the light from the hotel.

"Yes."

"Watch them," said the voice.

He heard nothing through the window's double-glazing. But suddenly, one after another, the three bottles broke and shattered, splintered glass flying the way that meant a high-velocity bullet.

"Just forget, Mr. Gaunt," said the voice mockingly, and the line went dead.

Gaunt put down the phone and stared out of the window. Nothing moved; then after a moment a car's lights showed about two hundred yards down the road and it drove away.

Closing the curtains, he sat down on the bed and contemplated the wad of kronur notes and the scattered papers. He'd been a potential threat to someone, because of what he might have been. Now they knew different, he was only worth scaring.

It was all very interesting, worth playing along with—till he found out why.

CHAPTER THREE

The bedside telephone wakened Jonathan Gaunt the next morning at 8 A.M. It was the alarm call he'd booked. He answered it still yawning, ordered a coffee and rolls breakfast to be sent up, then more or less crawled out of bed and went over to the window.

It was still dark as night outside, though the road was busy with traffic and lights seemed to be moving everywhere. It never really got dark in Iceland in mid-summer, but in winter, to compensate, dawn didn't arrive till mid-morning and daylight faded again in early afternoon. For a moment Gaunt watched the steady flow of cars heading in towards the glowing lights of Reykjavik. Then he looked down at the street immediately below.

The snowman was still there, the broken base of one of the bottles still on its head like a jagged miniature crown. That part had been no nightmare. Gaunt grimaced, realising he had had an untroubled night's sleep, knowing it was one of the crazy tricks his subconscious played when the real world was shaping rough.

He showered and shaved, dressed in tan slacks and a

blue wool shirt, got his old suede jacket from his bag, and
was pulling on his shoes when there was a knock at the
door. It opened and a maid, a blond teenage girl, came in
with his breakfast tray. But there was a man right behind
her, a burly six-footer in a brown sports suit. He gave
Gaunt a casual nod, waited till the maid had put down
the tray, gave her a smile which meant dismissal, then
firmly closed the door as she went out.

"Police, *Herra* Gaunt." The stranger, who had fair,
close-cropped hair, the inevitable blue eyes to go with it,
and a nose that looked as though it had been broken, was
in his mid-thirties. He tossed the coat he was carrying
onto a chair. "Inspector Gudnason—I'm attached to Headquarters here in Reykjavik."

"Mind proving it?" asked Gaunt, standing where he
was.

"*Ja*, more people should ask that." The faint smile
showed again and the man produced a warrant card, hesitated, then tossed it on the bed between them. Gaunt
glanced at the photograph, then the man, and handed it
back, satisfied.

"Well?"

"Now and again I pay . . . ah . . . a courtesy call on
some of the more interesting visitors to our country," said
Gudnason. He pointed towards the breakfast tray. "I had
the maid bring an extra coffee cup. Suppose I pour for
both of us while you find your passport?"

"The rolls stay mine," said Gaunt.

By the time he'd brought his passport from the bedside
drawer, Gudnason had the coffee poured. The policeman

checked carefully through the passport, rubbed a hand along his chin, then handed it back. Taking his coffee cup over to a chair, he sat down.

"Your breakfast," he suggested politely, then watched Gaunt take another chair over to the breakfast table and settle down. After a moment, he cleared his throat. "Your passport says you are a civil servant. Is this a working visit?"

"Yes." Gaunt chewed a mouthful of roll and washed it down with coffee. Both were good. "My department got caught up in settling the estate of the late James Douglas —you know about him?"

"*Ja.*" It came as a murmur of understanding, but Inspector Gudnason's face showed an odd disappointment. "And that's . . . ah . . . all?"

Still eating, Gaunt nodded. Rising again, he brought Gudnason the letter of authorisation from the Aberdeen lawyer, waited till the policeman had scanned it, then put it away.

"What's your problem, Inspector?" he asked. "Is it me— or do you just naturally go checking on anyone who visits Arkival Air?" He saw the man's surprise and grinned. "I heard Lief Ragnarson had a reputation, but my boss didn't send me over to set up any kind of bootlegging deal."

Gudnason grimaced. "I have a job to do. If you know about Ragnarson, then you can understand. He loses his partner, then a stranger arrives from Scotland, a stranger Ragnarson meets straight away—" He shrugged. "The sale of alcohol is a state monopoly here, except in hotels or restaurants, and prices come high. A smuggler who supplies cut-price liquor doesn't lack friends."

"Anywhere," agreed Gaunt. "But you've no real proof, right?"

"Not yet," admitted Gudnason. "A couple of times, nearly—and we know the stuff has to come in by fishing boat." He paused, taking a sip of coffee. "Did Ragnarson tell you what he planned to do last night?"

Gaunt nodded. "He and his wife were going to visit an aunt."

"Aunt Erna? We know her—an iron-faced hag who looks like she came off the prow of an old long-ship—and who'd lie her head off for him." He lifted his cup again, found it empty, and poured himself more without asking. "We heard a whisper there was to be landing last night from a trawler and the coastguards had a radar watch on her. She twice seemed to be coming in, towards Snaefellanes, on the west coast. But the whisper must have got back—each time she veered out again, didn't as much as stop."

"My interest stays James Douglas," said Gaunt.

"He was mine too," said Gudnason. "I handled the investigation into his death, even if I only understood half what the radio experts told me. You heard how it happened?"

Gaunt nodded.

"Part of the reason was the power of the transmitter in that Arkival Air office," said Gudnason. "It can blast out a signal far beyond what they need to talk to their aircraft flying around Iceland—it's strong enough to contact

America or Europe as if they're next door. They could be in direct contact with a fishing boat from the moment it left Norway or England or anywhere else."

"But Douglas's death was an accident?" persisted Gaunt.

"It looked that way," said Gudnason. "I—well, let's say I couldn't prove anything else, and I'd have been happy to try." Setting down his cup, he walked over to the window and looked out into the darkness. "It's unlikely, but if you need my kind of help while you're here, let me know."

"As soon as I get through with Ragnarson. I'll be on the next plane out," Gaunt told him. "That's if I don't get snowed in."

"There's a thaw forecast," Gudnason assured him. "By tonight, most of this should have gone. Our Tourist Board says winter in Iceland is milder than in Chicago."

"Chicago should sue them," said Gaunt.

Gudnason shook his head, said good-bye, and left. As the door closed, Gaunt lit a cigarette and frowned, knowing how near he'd come to telling the policeman what had happened the previous night. But he hadn't—and he still wasn't sure why not.

He checked the coffee-pot, found it was empty, and swore softly. Chewing the remnants of a roll, he finished dressing and was almost ready to leave when the telephone rang. He answered and it was the desk clerk from the hotel lobby who was calling.

"Mr. Gaunt, there is a lady here wanting to see you," said the clerk. "She says you know her—a *Fru* Bennett."

"I'll be right down," said Gaunt, surprised.

He checked his pockets and was ready to leave when the telephone rang again. Shrugging, he lifted the receiver; then his lips tightened as the voice from the previous night sounded in his ear.

"I hear you've had a visitor, Mr. Gaunt—from the police." The voice was cool and casual. "Did you invite him?"

"No." Gaunt took a long breath. "But it might have been a good idea."

He heard an amused chuckle. "I half-expected it might happen. And you kept to our little bargain of last night?"

"Yes," said Gaunt. "But get off my back or I might change my mind."

He hung up without waiting for a reply, glared at the telephone, then left his room and went down to the lobby.

Chris Bennett's coppery hair and leather coat made her easy to spot, even though a bus-load of airline travellers had just arrived and were milling around, booking in. She had been talking to a Scandinavian Air Services stewardess but said a quick good-bye and broke off as he came over.

"Good morning." She greeted him with a friendly nod, eyeing his casual dress and apparently approving. "Lief Ragnarson sent me over, Mr. Gaunt. He thought you could maybe use a car while you're here—"

"And a driver?" asked Gaunt hopefully.

"Wheels only. You have an International Licence, I suppose?"

Gaunt nodded.

"Good," she said briskly. "It's outside."

She led the way out of the hotel and across the snow of the car park, where the chill morning darkness was beginning to hold a first hint of grey. They stopped beside a dark blue station wagon, a French-built Matra festooned with extra lights, aerials, and protective bump-grilles. But beneath the cosmetics, Gaunt knew the make. It was a tough, go-anywhere vehicle with a rugged four-cylinder engine which was the next best thing to a fully-fledged safari car.

"There can't be too many of these around," he said mildly. "Who uses it?"

Chris Bennett shook her head. "Right now, nobody, Mr. Gaunt. Jamie Douglas had it imported and drove it most of the time. Since he died, it hasn't been out of the Arkival hangar." She shrugged. "Lief thought you might as well borrow it."

"Tell him I'm grateful, and do me a favour—people call me Jonathan." He took the keys from her, then asked, "Can I give you a lift back?"

"No." She hesitated. "I'm going to the harbour on an errand for Lief. But I'll get a cab."

"No way." He gestured towards the passenger door. "I like harbours—and I could use a guide."

For a moment she seemed ready to protest. Then she smiled instead, nodded, and they got aboard.

Purring in towards the city through the growing predawn twilight, the Matra station wagon gave the impression of being glad to be back at work after its enforced idleness. As a guide, Chris Bennett was quietly self-assured. She pointed out an occasional feature but most of the time left Gaunt to see for himself.

They passed a brightly lit and busy open-air swimming pool where the steaming water came straight from an underground hot spring. Long, large-bore pipelines snaked everywhere, bringing vast quantities of that same Icelandic natural resource from geysers and steam-holes to warm the capital's homes and office blocks.

At first, Reykjavik's suburban fringe and inner circle of houses and apartment blocks, hotels, and supermarkets were like those of any other city except that the corrugated iron roofs highlighted the fact that wood was wealth on a virtually treeless island. But, as the station wagon neared the centre, the old city took over. The buildings were dull, dark stone, squat, designed to resist the winter hardships of an earlier time even if bright with modern paint colours. Here and there a statue or a shopfront name acted as a sharp reminder of the ninth-century Vikings who had braved an ocean in their tiny craft to tame and settle a land of glacial ice and volcanic fire.

Told to take a right turn, Gaunt drove round a square which contained the tiny Icelandic Parliament building, smaller than the average European town hall; passed a Lutheran cathedral; then a moment later saw the vast sprawl of Reykjavik harbour appear ahead.

They parked at the edge of a flood-lit quayside lined with an armada of fishing boats and got out, the scent of fish and diesel oil meeting them like a wave. Fishing was Iceland's life-blood, and it showed—solid ranks of trawlers were tied up along the north-east arm of the harbour, punctuated here and there by the slim grey shape of a coastguard gunboat. An inner basin was freighter territory, busy with tall masts and funnels. But the west side, where they'd stopped, was again exclusively fishing-boat territory, a bustle of catches being swung ashore, of ice being shovelled from trucks into fish-holds, of sea-booted crewmen working and gossiping.

"Where now?" asked Gaunt, looking around.

"Around here, somewhere." Chris Bennett frowned at the nearest flotilla of boats, some brightly lit, others mere dark outlines creaking at their moorings in the greyness. "According to Lief, anyway. She's a local boat, the *Orva*."

"Newly in?" Gaunt said it almost sharply, his interest roused, remembering Gudnarson and the policeman's story.

This morning sometime." Suddenly, she brightened. "There it is—the boat with the zebra-striped wheelhouse. Now let's hope Sven Muller's still aboard—he's the skipper, a friend of Lief's."

They threaded their way across the wet slush, stepping over mooring lines and dodging round piled fish boxes. The *Orva*, a medium-sized trawler with more rust than paintwork, had a sad rag of an Icelandic flag hanging limp at her stern and was third out in a line of boats tied to the quayside. A solitary deckhand was working at the edge of her fish-hold and looked up as Chris hailed him. He waved in understanding, then ambled into the zebra-striped wheelhouse.

Within a minute, Sven Muller scrambled over the boats

and joined them on the quayside. He was an unshaven, middle-aged medium-sized man in an old blue suit, a greasy cap clinging to the back of his head. But he had an infectious, gap-toothed grin which he turned to Gaunt briefly after greeting Chris. Then, taking her by the arm, he led her a few paces away. Gaunt watched the girl hand over an envelope, which Muller tucked away. That done, Muller spoke to her again, softly, finishing with a laugh before he turned and made his way back to his trawler.

"Finished?" asked Gaunt as Chris returned.

"Yes." She wrinkled her nose. "That man must have the best stock of dirty stories in the North Atlantic—believe me, I'm not repeating that one."

"Next time, tell him you know a collector." Gaunt nodded towards the trawler. "I thought Lief Ragnarson was out of the fishing business."

"He is and he isn't," she said. "His family used to own a couple of boats and run a boat-repair yard. He still has connections and so does Anna—she's from the same kind of background."

"Any idea what goes on between him and Muller?" asked Gaunt as casually as he could.

"No." Her manner cooled a fraction. "I'd say it wasn't any of my business."

"Or mine? Sorry. Ragnarson interests me, that's all—he's quite a character."

"He is—and not as tough as he makes out." Chris Bennett flicked back a loose strand of her long, coppery hair, paused, and looked out across the harbour for a moment.

"I didn't mean to snarl. But I've got my own set of rules. One of them is that people either tell me things or they don't—life's simpler if I leave it that way."

"And that's how you want it?"

"Yes." It came quietly, almost bitterly. "I learned."

"Lief told me." Gaunt took her arm and brought her gently round to face him. "People survive it, Chris. I found that out for myself. You don't forget, but one day you wake up and discover you can start living again."

"Maybe." She looked at him closely, as if seeing him for the first time. "I didn't know. I—" She paused and gave a sudden shiver. "It's getting cold, Jonathan. Let's get back to the car."

They went back along the quayside towards the Matra. A slim, bespectacled figure who had been standing inspecting it turned, saw them, stayed there, waiting. It was Harald Nordur, wearing a thigh-length quilted jacket and a fur cap. Under the powerful lights, a quizzical expression showed on his sallow face.

"*Morgen*," he said. "I wondered when I saw James Douglas's fun machine down here." He glanced from Chris to Gaunt, the metal frames of his spectacles glinting. "Maybe I should have guessed. We met yesterday, Mr. Gaunt, at Arkival Air."

"But didn't quite get round to saying hello," said Gaunt. "Still, Ragnarson told me about you."

"In the mood he was in?" A fractional smile twitched the adventure camp director's lips. He switched his attention to Chris for a moment. "You are well, *Fru* Bennett?"

She gave a cool nod but said nothing.

"Good." Producing a thin brown cheroot from a top pocket, Nordur snapped a flame from a slim gold lighter and used it. "You can save me a telephone call. When you see your boss, tell him I've had to change my plans for this afternoon. I can't make the round trip flight to Alfaburg when your people make that freight delivery. Say I'll be in touch later. You'll remember?"

"I'll try," she said sarcastically.

"*Takk.*" Unperturbed, Nordur turned to Gaunt. "Did Ragnarson tell you about Alfaburg?"

Gaunt nodded. "Adventure training—I've heard of it before."

"We're not unique, except maybe in surroundings," said Nordur, drawing placidly on his cheroot. "The camp is deep in the *obyggdir*—lava rock desert, Mr. Gaunt, as divorced from civilised terms as the far side of the moon. In fact, Alfaburg is one of the locations the American NASA people used for their space training programme. We stepped in after they abandoned it."

"From spacemen to junior executives sounds drastic enough," said Gaunt. "What do you do? Hand out gold stars for trying?"

"Something like that." Nordur showed slight annoyance, his mouth tightening. He paused while a heavy truck laden with fish boxes rumbled past them, then used the cheroot like a pointer. "Believe me, if you disorientate a man away from all things familiar and subject him to controlled stress the way we can at Alfaburg then the results can be valuable—that's why plenty of major business organisations use us."

"I'll take your word for it," said Gaunt. "My Boy Scout days are over." He glanced at Chris, standing silent beside them and exhibiting a pointed disinterest. Then he asked Nordur, "What's happening to the new arrivals who got in yesterday?"

"Settling in," answered Nordur. "The camp staff will make sure they don't get lost and I'll join them in a day or so when the real work begins. I've some business in Reykjavik that has to come first." He frowned at his wristwatch as he spoke. "Including an appointment due now. But I'll probably see you again."

He nodded good-bye, turned on his heel, and walked away. A grey Volvo coupe was parked a short distance away and Nordur got in on the passenger side. It started up and passed them a moment later, the man behind the wheel a lean-faced individual with full lips and close-cropped fair hair.

"Who's that with him?" asked Gaunt as the Volvo disappeared along the harbourside.

"Gunnar Bjargson, Nordur's man in Reykjavik. They rent what they call an office in an old warehouse block not far from here. It's just a couple of rooms and Bjargson lives and works there."

Gaunt nodded, her answer having given him at least part of a reason for Nordur being around the harbour area.

"And neither of them rates as your favourite character?"

"No," she admitted.

"Why?"

"Bjargson I just don't like. I let Nordur take me out once—and once was enough."

She left it at that and Gaunt had the feeling he'd be wise to do the same. He nodded towards the station wagon, set the heater going the moment they were aboard, but didn't start the engine for a moment.

"As long as it's personal," he said softly. "I thought maybe it had something to do with Jamie Douglas." He met her startled glance and gave a sideways grin. "I still want to hear more about that, even if Lief Ragnarson thinks you're crazy."

"Maybe I am." The words came sharply. "But Harald Nordur isn't part of it."

Silently, Gaunt took out his cigarettes, lit two with the facia lighter, gave the girl one, and waited. For almost a minute things stayed that way, neither of them saying anything.

"Officially, I'm the last person known to have seen Jamie Douglas alive," she said reluctantly. "I was still in the office when he arrived that night and he more or less threw me out, told me to go home."

"You think he was expecting someone?"

"I thought so." She bit her lip. "It doesn't sound much to anyone else, I know. But I had the feeling he was nervous and—yes, excited at the same time. I'd never seen him that way before."

"He didn't give any reason for wanting you out?"

"No." She looked at the cigarette in her fingers almost distastefully and stubbed it out in the dashboard ashtray. "You'd better know the other thing I told the police. I told them I thought he was carrying a gun that night. He took off his flying jacket and tossed it on a desk. Something fell out of the pocket. He grabbed it. I only got a glance, but—" She stopped there.

"What did the police say?"

"That they didn't find a gun. That all the evidence pointed to an accident with the transmitter aerial."

But even the best of cops weren't infallible; accidents could be rigged, an aerial broken, a switch thrown— Gaunt frowned at the steering wheel.

"Had he any real enemies?"

Chris shook her head. "None I knew about."

"How did he get along with Nordur?"

"All right. Anyway, Harald Nordur was at the Alfaburg camp when it happened," she said. "He flew back from there the next day. Now can we stop talking about it?"

"Yes." Leaning forward, Gaunt started the engine. "But I'd like the rest of the guided tour. How about it?"

She took a moment, then gave a slight smile and nodded.

Dawn arrived as they left the harbour area. A pale yellow sun fringed by a faint blue corona shone down on the city as the Matra's tyres splashed through melting slush and great puddles of draining water—and the streets were crowded. In Reykjavik every man, woman, and child seemed to make the most of their few precious hours of winter daylight.

For about an hour Grant let Chris Bennett give the orders and they cruised around, past the American statue to Leif Ericson who reached North America in the tenth century, round squares and gardens, briefly sight-seeing outside the National Museum, making a coffee-stop near the state broadcasting studios—where Icelandic TV worked an eleven-month year and closed down in July for its annual holiday.

Then, a little later, they pulled in at a hilltop viewpoint with the whole Reykjavik peninsula spread below them, backed by mountains, a blue shimmer on the horizon marking the outline of the Snaefell glacier, sixty miles distant.

"We'll need to go back soon," said Chris, pointing to the dashboard clock. "Anyway, that's most of the instant tour—had enough?"

"Yes, for now." Gaunt settled back behind the wheel, his eyes on a string of half a dozen tiny specks coming in across the water, deep-sea trawlers returning to port. Since he and Chris had left the harbour area any conversation between them had been light and general and he was reluctant to end the self-imposed truce. "I'll make soothing noises to Ragnarson—tell him I kidnapped you or something."

"He told me not to rush back," she said demurely. "A happy Mr. Gaunt is good business for Arkival Air."

"Softening me up? It worked. He's a good judge of character, your friendly bootlegger—"

"Bootlegger?"

"I was thinking aloud," said Gaunt. "Anyway, what did he say about tonight?"

She shook her head. "That's after hours."

"So?" He rubbed a finger round the rim of the steering

wheel. "You could eat out on my expense account, choose where, spend the British taxpayer's money—Iceland's revenge for the Cod War."

"Put it that way and I can't refuse." She sounded pleased. Then she saw the dashboard clock again and winced. "Let's move. I promised I'd deliver you back by noon."

They made it to the airport only a couple of minutes late and parked at the Arkival Air office. Crossing over from the station wagon, Gaunt paused for his first real daylight view of the airfield layout, snow gone from the runways and the tarmac wet and glistening. There were too many light aircraft parked around the perimeter area to even attempt to count them. But the busy roar of engines warming made him glance round as an old tri-motor Fokker began rolling to take its place in a queue of aircraft waiting to take off while the sleek silver shape of a short-haul jet came whining in to land.

"Market-day," said Chris, joining him. "In the trade, we call a lot of those flights 'housewife specials'—if you live up-country you fly in for the week's shopping."

He nodded, remembering Ragnarson's report. In a country where there were no railways, only one real road around the coast, and little more than lava-tracks inland, flying housewives had to be accepted as the norm.

"Thanks." He winked at her. "You just pushed my terms up ten per cent."

They went into the main office, where the big, blond shape of Anna Jorgensdottir bustled forward to meet them.

"Lief is out in the hangar, helping Pete Close tie on wings or something," she said cheerfully. "Chris, you go tell him." She watched Chris depart, then considered Gaunt thoughtfully. "You look like you both enjoyed your morning, *Herra* Gaunt. I'm glad, for Chris's sake. More than anything else, that girl needs—" She paused, for a moment something close to a blush showed on her pleasant middle-aged face, then she shook her head. "No, I think I leave that to you to work out."

Lief Ragnarson joined them a moment later, wiping his hands on a rag. He nodded to Gaunt, slapped his wife on the rump, then beckoned them to follow. A desk in a small room off the main office had been covered with a clean white tablecloth and every available inch of cloth seemed filled with plates of cold food, from chunky open sandwiches to chicken legs and lobster.

"Anna and I never eat much at mid-day," said Ragnarson. "So we thought maybe we could have a small snack with you here and talk business at the same time." He paused and rubbed his chin apologetically. "But maybe if you feel hungry—"

"This looks like it'll do," said Gaunt.

They sat round the desk, Ragnarson uncapping three bottles of German beer which had to have come into the country bootleg style. But neither of his hosts commented and Gaunt took their lead and began to eat.

"Okay," said Ragnarson, demolishing a chicken leg and already reaching for another. "We can start. You read those papers?"

Gaunt nodded. "I'll take your figures on trust. But I'll

need them verified later, tax certificates, bank state-
ments—"

"*Ja*, I know." Ragnarson pointed at his wife. "Anna's
department. I maybe make the money, but she's the one
who can count." As Anna Jorgensdottir beamed, Ragnarson winked. "She spends most of it, anyway."

It was the start of a long, toughening session with
Gaunt finding two needle-sharp minds teamed ready to
meet each question he raised. From aircraft depreciation
and engine hours to bank account interest and loans,
checking issues as varied as hangar rental and aviation
fuel agreements, he gradually worked his way through
the mental check-list he'd prepared. Ragnarson and his
wife talked and ate, new bottles of beer appeared and
were emptied, and then, surprisingly, it reached an end.

"No more, *Herra* Gaunt?" Anna Jorgensdottir closed
the last of the pile of account ledgers she'd been using
and gave a quick glance at her husband as Gaunt shook
his head. "Then . . . ah—"

"I want to sell, you're interested in buying." Gaunt
crumpled the sheet of paper he'd been using for scribbled
calculations, tossed it into a bucket, and sat back. "I
reckon Jamie Douglas's share in Arkival Air could be
worth forty thousand pounds—"

"Eh?" Ragnarson blanched. "But—"

"Hold on." Gaunt frowned at him. "I said could.
There's a legal mess back in Scotland and my Department
want it sorted out, whatever the cost. I'll take twenty-
eight thousand sterling, cash on the nail."

Ragnarson swallowed hard and turned to his wife
"Anna, in kronur—"

She was already scribbling. A smile on her face, she shoved a slip of paper in front of the man. He looked at it, then at Gaunt, swallowed again, and glanced at his wife. She nodded vigorously.

"You have a deal," said Ragnarson hoarsely. "But I will need time—a couple of days, okay?"

"Forty-eight hours and you pay the legal costs this end," said Gaunt. He was handing them a bargain, not a total giveaway but still a better deal than they could have hoped for. So a slight squeeze on the tail helped salve his conscience as far as the Department was concerned. "We say nothing about the deal until it's completed."

Ragnarson sealed the bargain with a bone-crushing handshake. While Gaunt was recovering, Anna Jorgens-dottir gave her husband an affectionate bearhug, then turned towards Gaunt with a similar intention.

He was saved as the door swung open and Pete Close stuck his thin, gloomy face round the edge.

"The truck with that freight for Alfaburg has arrived," he said. "Want to check before we load, Lief?"

"*Takk*, okay. I'll come." Ragnarson grimaced at Gaunt. "This won't take long. Help yourself to another beer. Anna, you better come too."

They went out. Left alone, Gaunt lit a cigarette, then went out into the deserted main office, looked around, and sighed. His official role was going smoothly; two more days and the folks at Buckingham Palace would have been eased out of their comic cuts dilemma. But the rest worried him, gave him the feeling that the edge of a curtain had been drawn back just enough to send some particularly nasty secrets scurrying in confusion.

Though the Remembrancer would have told him to keep his nose out of it. He shrugged, drew on his cigarette again, and began a casual exploration of the office area. A door lying open near the back attracted him. He looked into a darkened room, found the light switch, snapped it on, then whistled under his breath.

He'd found the Arkival Air radio transmitter. It was even bigger than he'd anticipated, a bank of metal cabinets, dials and relay switches for the moment silent and lifeless but still constituting a system layout capable of punching out a massive signal strength.

The kind that had seared the life out of Jamie Douglas. Lips still puckered, he was puzzling over the layout and trying to relate it to his slender experience of military sets when he heard footsteps behind him and turned.

"*Herra* Gaunt." Anne Jorgensdottir came in, moving in the light, easy way he found so surprising for a woman of her bulk. She smiled at him then glanced at the transmitter. "You know about these things?"

He shook his head. "Very little."

"It murdered Jamie." Anna Jorgensdottir spoke in a flat, controlled voice. "Lief and I—well, we're excited. But it is easy to forget why." She paused, her mood changing. "Still, I can show you why he was proud of it."

Stepping forward, she hesitated a moment, then threw a few switches. The receiver side warmed to life with a low hum, the static growing from the loudspeaker as the woman spun a tuning dial.

"Telephone bands," she explained, as a varied jumble of voices came blasting into the room. "The island has four radio-telephone stations, all tied to the land-line system. Most of our smaller villages link up that way. The shipping and fishing bands are here"—her thick fingers spun the dial again, through a band of snarling static, then that ended as she closed a switch—"and then we have the aircraft high frequencies."

A new voice came piping into the room, the accent American and more distant, a Pan Am 707 flight en route to Europe talking to Paris from mid-Atlantic. Gaunt nodded thoughtfully.

"But local air traffic will use a VHF channel?" he asked.

"*Ja*, I'll show you." She switched again, frowning in concentration. "Jamie was our expert at this—but at least I'm better at it than Lief." New voices filled the room and she fiddled with the tuning dial. "Around here on the dial you get all kinds of people, not just aircraft. Wait"—she chuckled as a low, flat voice talking in Icelandic rasped from the receiver—"I thought so. This is the Alfaburg camp in the *obyggdir*. They're talking direct to their Reykjavik office about the freight we're taking up."

"What's in the load?" asked Gaunt as the voice muttered on.

"Food, spare parts, the usual . . ." She paused as another voice replied on the same frequency.

Gaunt froze. The conversation was still in Icelandic but the new voice was unmistakable, the same cool, precise tones he'd heard over the telephone in his room. He had a vivid mental picture of the snowman and the shattering bottles.

"Who's on now?" he demanded.

Anna Jorgensdottir blinked. "Just their office in Reykjavik."

"But who's talking?" persisted Gaunt. "Do you know?"

She nodded. "Gunnar Bjargson, their manager." Her hand reached for the dial again. "Maybe I can find something more interesting."

"No, don't bother." Gaunt tried to sound casually disinterested while his thoughts raced. If Bjargson was the man who had threatened him and Bjargson worked for Harald Nordur— He left it there, seeing the woman had switched off the equipment. "Thanks for the demonstration. Anna, do you remember what frequency Jamie Douglas was trying to transmit on when he died?"

"*Nei*, but it looked like he'd just switched on at random." Her lips tightened. "The police hoped it would be the fishing waveband, of course. I think you know what they say about Lief—"

"Which couldn't possibly be true," he said with a mock solemnity. "How was Aunt Erna when you saw her?"

Her eyes widened, then she laughed. "*Herra* Gaunt, maybe you guess too much. Like I told Chris, you also have a persuasive way that probably gets you most things." She winked deliberately. "If I was maybe ten years younger, it would get you anything."

"As much as ten?" Gaunt gave her a grin, but his mind was on another track. "Will Lief still be out in the hangar?"

She nodded and he went there. A small delivery truck was drawn up beside one of the twin-engined Cessnas and Ragnarson was helping two men carry an assortment of cartons from the truck to the aircraft where Pete Close was doing the actual loading. Chris was there too, keeping a check on the cartons as they went aboard. Tapping

Ragnarson on the shoulder, Gaunt beckoned him out of the line.

"There's a spare seat on this flight. Mind if I fill it, round-trip?" he asked.

"Well . . ." Ragnarson hesitated. "That damn Nordur doesn't allow visitors unless he says okay first."

"That's his privilege," said Gaunt. "Mine is I happen to represent the owners of almost half of this outfit—remember?"

"So you go," agreed Ragnarson.

"Thanks." Gaunt stuck his hands in his pockets, watching the loading for a moment. "Lief, what happened to Jamie Douglas's personal belongings?"

Ragnarson grimaced and scratched his chin in embarrassed style.

"We had a problem," he admitted. "There wasn't much in his apartment. I gave away most of it and passed any personal papers to our lawyer. If that was wrong—"

Gaunt shook his head. "I'm not worried. Was he flying the day he died?"

"*Ja.*" Ragnarson answered without hesitating. "He made a trip to the Alfaburg camp that morning." He frowned. "You know, there's not much daylight left. You won't see much on the trip."

"Call it an experience," said Gaunt. "It'll fill in time."

CHAPTER FOUR

The pilot for the Alfaburg flight was a young dark-haired Dane, Jarl Hansen, and he strolled in just as Ragnarson and his team finished loading the Cessna.

"I like company," he said, as Ragnarson introduced Gaunt and they shook hands. "*Ja*, most of all on a trip like this—otherwise, I feel like a damn truck driver." Taking the flight schedule from Ragnerson, he eyed the loaded aircraft with something like suspicion. In addition to the regular baggage compartment in the nose the rear seating area had been stripped and filled. "Okay, let's try and get her off the ground."

Chris was in the background. Gaunt gave her a wave, climbed aboard into the co-pilot seat, and waited while Hansen made a fast, thorough job of the pre-flight check list. The big, three-bladed propellors began spinning as the twin Continental engines fired. Then, winking at him, Hansen taxied the aircraft out of the hangar and they moved out towards the runway.

They had to wait for take-off clearance and Hansen grunted as the reason, the other red Arkival Air Cessna, murmured in and touched down.

"Mattison," he said. "You met him yet?"

Gaunt shook his head.

"About fifty, Icelandic, and dumb as an ox," said Hansen. "Lief usually gives him the Alfaburg flights but this time he was sent out with a package of tourists to the Westman Islands." His mouth puckered with amusement as the other aircraft taxied off the runway. "Well, at least he found his way back."

They took off a moment later climbing fast, making a tight north-east turn with Reykjavik under the port wing and the rays of the setting sun glinting on the fuselage. Whistling tunelessly, Hansen corrected the Cessna's trim, then kept her climbing. When they levelled out, they were at eight thousand feet, the Cessna steady at her two hundred miles an hour cruising speed. Down below, the patchwork of snow-streaked farmland was already giving way to more snow and lifeless rock and the occasional upthrust of a dead volcanic cone.

"What's our route?" asked Gaunt above the throbbing engine noise.

"Pretty direct." Passing over a clipboard-mounted map, Hansen pointed to the vast blue-white mass of a glacier beginning to fill the greying horizon. "That's Langjokull. We keep to her right, cross the Hofsjokull glacier after that, then it's pretty much a business of lose height and land." He frowned at the light. "But you won't see much of anything."

The Dane was right. A few more minutes and the world faded through grey to a moonlit darkness in which the blue glint of Langjokull remained as a pallid glitter.

Then it faded behind them to be replaced by empty, snow-covered terrain for a spell before the next great ice barrier, the Hofsjokull, began to take shape. Looking down, Gaunt caught himself imagining what a forced landing anywhere below might mean.

"One thing about Alfaburg is we'll have a fast turnround," said Hansen cheerfully. "They don't exactly roll out the welcome mat, but they won't keep you hanging about—and I've a date back in town tonight."

"Who heads the reception committee?" asked Gaunt.

"Usually the chief instructor, Franz Renotti—he's Swiss and the type that chews nails and spits rust." Hansen paused, checking the instrument panel and making a slight course correction. The Cessna had begun to buck a little as they met the updraughts from the glacier now directly below. "The other three aren't so bad—there's a local guide called Petursson and the other two talk like Americans, wherever they come from."

"And the students?"

"We fly them in like lambs to the slaughter," said Hansen dryly. "But they volunteer, don't they?"

Ten minutes later, clear of the Hofsjokull, the Cessna began to lose height and Hansen used his radio. A voice murmured back in his earphones and he kept bringing the aircraft lower, whistling tunelessly again as he concentrated on the dark landscape ahead. Then he gave a satisfied grunt as a twin line of lights came to life almost directly ahead.

"We're there," he announced with a mild satisfaction. "Alfaburg—in Icelandic, it means something like 'the valley of the elves,' though they're the hairiest bunch of elves I've ever seen."

They touched down on a narrow, bumpy airstrip, turned and taxied back to halt beside a low, mostly darkened huddle of huts. A small group of men who had been waiting came towards the aircraft as Gaunt and Hansen climbed out into a bitter cold with crisp snow underfoot. At the same time a jeep left the shadow of one of the huts and drove across, headlights blazing.

Hansen spent a moment talking to a parka-clad figure who was obviously in charge of the reception party, then brought him over.

"This is Franz Renotti, the chief instructor," he said. "He says if you want to go over to the office and grab some coffee, his boys will get on with unloading."

Renotti, a bearded hawk-faced man with no kind of welcome in his eyes, grunted agreement.

"We have no facilities for visitors," he said curtly, in heavily accented English. "No time for guided tours either—you understand?" As Gaunt nodded, the man beckoned another of the parka-muffled figures. "One of the students will take you over."

Gaunt followed his guide the short distance across the snow to one of the nearest huts. Shoving open the door, they went into a brightly lit, sparsely furnished room which obviously served as a general office. A bottled gas stove was shoving out heat and a coffee-pot was bubbling on top. His guide, a young man with swarthy features, fetched a mug from a cupboard, filled it with coffee, and brought it over.

"Thanks." Taking the mug, Gaunt nodded towards the pot. "Joining me?"

"Hell no, mister." The student smiled at him. "Do that an' Renotti will skin me. Out here, a work detail is a work detail."

Giving a mock salute, his guide went back out into the darkness. Sipping his coffee, Gaunt looked around. A noticeboard held duty rosters and lecture details, a neat stack of skis were piled against the wall, and a scarred table served as a desk. He raised an eyebrow at the sight of an automatic rifle sharing space in a gunrack with a couple of shotguns, then turned as the door swung open again.

A new parka-clad figure struggled in, kicked the door shut behind him, thumped a heavy wooden box on the desk, then faced Gaunt.

"Thinking of joining us, Mr. Gaunt?" he asked breezily, a grin spreading on his freckled face. "After this lot, Edinburgh's going to look like the Promised Land when I get back."

"Adam Lawton—what the hell are you doing out here?" Gaunt stared at the red-haired man who was already soaking up some of the stove's warmth. Adam Lawton's father now drove a taxi around Edinburgh, but before that he had been Gaunt's first platoon sergeant. "The last time I met your old man, he said you'd qualified as a surveyor."

"Right." Lawton stayed close to the stove. "I'm working with Commonwealth Engineering."

"And they packed you out here?" Commonwealth was

among the biggest civil engineering outfits in Scotland, the kind that took on contracts anywhere there was money to be made. "Does that mean you're good—or did they just want you out of their hair?"

"Hold on." Lawton crossed to a window, eased the blind open a fraction, peered out, then closed it again. "That basket Renotti's still busy at the plane, so I can hide for a moment." He drew out cigarettes and lit one quickly. "This is no luxury hotel, Mr. Gaunt. I've been here two days, first batch of the new course, and they throw you straight in—we've had our tails chased A.M. till P.M., then P.M. till A.M. Tonight we're supposed to go sleeping in snowholes up a mountain."

"It's character-forming, like castor oil," said Gaunt. "You're a budding executive, remember?"

"Me?" Lawton shook his head, then paused, embarrassed. "Well, I suppose I can tell you, though I'm supposed to keep my mouth shut about it. Commonwealth have got themselves a major new hydro-electric construction contract in Northern Iceland—so big the Icelandics are talking about exporting surplus power to Europe by submarine cable. The deal's being announced soon; they've put a site team together for it, and I'm one of them. But I've never been anywhere wilder than a day trip to Glasgow so—"

"So sending you on this makes sense." Gaunt realised that the redheaded youngster amounted to an unexpected bonus. "Adam, what do you make of the set-up here?"

"Stand back from things, and I suppose I'm enjoying it," admitted Lawton. He grinned. "I've teamed up with a mad Spaniard called Juan—the character who brought you over here."

"How about instructors?"

"Hard men, but they act like they know their stuff." Lawton frowned, sniffed, and moved a step away from the stove. The tail of his parka was beginning to singe. "Mind you, we haven't got totally going yet—the other half of my group only arrived yesterday. They seem all right." He shrugged. "There's another class who have been here longer, but they're off limits as far as we're concerned."

"You don't mix?" asked Gaunt, surprised. He glanced at the time-tables on the board. "I'd have thought—"

"You won't find them there," said Lawton. "Our mob call them the leper colony. They've got their own bunkhouse, their own lecture room—and if we're in camp, they're out; if they're in camp, we're out. It gets a bit weird."

"Same instructors?"

Drawing on his cigarette, Lawton nodded.

"You must have seen them around," suggested Gaunt.

"Once or twice," said Lawton. "There are eight of them, older than us, almost middle-aged—you know, heading into their thirties."

"Thanks," said Gaunt.

Then the hut door swung open, slamming back on its hinges. A tall man in a dark waterproof suit, a battered cap jammed on his head, came in and scowled at Lawton, thumbing out at the darkness.

"You," he snapped. "Move. Warm your backside later."

His eyes flickered in Gaunt's direction, then he went out again, leaving the door still open.

"Damn." Hastily, Lawton stubbed his cigarette. "That's Garram, one of the instructors. Garram the Gorilla, we call him. Sorry, that's it."

"Hold a moment." Gaunt got between him and the doorway. "Adam, where are this special group located?"

"Behind here and to your left." Lawton eased past him as he spoke. "It's a concrete blockhouse of a thing—something left over from when the American NASA people were here."

He vanished, closing the door behind him. Lips pursed, Gaunt stood where he was for a moment, than laid down the coffee mug, went over to the window, and peered out round the edge of the blind. The task of unloading the Cessna was still under way, some of the men shifting crates over to the jeep, a couple carrying smaller cartons directly towards the huts.

Instinct, doubt, and curiosity in almost equal proportions had brought him out to Alfaburg. Now, though still with no real answers, he felt certain he was right and that whatever was going on had to involve this ludicrous, bleak group of huts in the middle of an emptiness of cold, lava-rock desert.

Quickly, he crossed to the door, opened it a crack, checked the men were still busy at the aircraft, then slipped out into the night and closed the door as he left. The air was chill and the snow crunched under his feet as he kept to the shadows thrown by the huts and followed Adam Lawton's scanty directions.

They were enough. The concrete blockhouse stood stark and square in the moonlight, it and a single small hut set back a little way from the rest of the camp. He crossed a strip of open ground towards it cautiously, noting the tall aerial mast which rose from the flat roof and the few edges of light which showed at some of its high, narrow windows.

There was only one obvious door and a sign was attached to the concrete wall beside it. As he got closer, shivering as the cold penetrated his clothing, Gaunt paused and read the warning: OUT OF BOUNDS AT ALL TIMES UNLESS AUTHORISED. The same message was repeated in equally large letters in German, French, and Icelandic.

It seemed a good enough invitation. Reaching the door, he gently tried the handle and found it locked. He checked round the rest of the outside without success except for hearing the faint sound of music coming from somewhere inside.

Then a new sound reached his ears, the growl of the jeep's engine. Gaunt hugged a corner wall as it came into sight, headlamps blazing, and stopped close to the blockhouse door. There was only one man aboard and he got out, went to the door, and hammered on it with his fist.

The door opened. As light spilled out, Gaunt recognised the jeep driver was Garram the Gorilla; he had obviously been expected. Three men came out of the blockhouse, pulling on jackets as they emerged. With Garram's help, they began unloading crates from the jeep and carrying them into the blockhouse, talking as they worked, their voices too low for Gaunt to know whàt they were saying.

One of the men laughed. At the same instant, a crate slipped—and the laugh altered to an almost terrified cry of warning as the edge of the crate hit the ground. The group of men stood as if turned to stone for a moment, then the same man laughed again, nervously this time, and they restarted.

There was only one crate left on the jeep. Deciding it wasn't wise to wait, Gaunt eased further back into the shadows, then quickly headed back the way he'd come. Reaching the office hut, he opened the door and stepped inside.

"You were told to stay," said a cold, angry voice.

Franz Renotti stood in the middle of the room, his bearded face stony, hands hanging like waiting talons. Beside him, looking slightly worried, was Jarl Hansen.

"We're . . . uh . . . finished," said the young pilot almost apologetically. "Nobody knew where you were."

"Sorry." Gaunt beamed at. Renotti and deliberately crossed to the stove to warm himself. "I thought I'd take a walk around, stretch my legs a little before I got stuffed back into that plane." Turning his back to the stove, he gave a contented sigh and added, "Not much to see, is there? But I wouldn't mind coming back in daylight."

"It's safer then," said Renotti grimly, his hands relaxing as he spoke. "We have reasons for our rules. There are drainage ditches, other hazards—you were foolish." He glanced at Hansen. "You are ready?"

Hansen nodded and led the way out. When they

reached the Cessna, the last few crates and cartons lying on the ground were being cleared away by the student work-party. Adam Lawton was one of them but kept well clear as Hansen followed Gaunt aboard.

The bearded figure of Renotti stayed close, watching until the engines fired to life. Then, as the aircraft began to move, he stepped back.

"Like I warned you," said Hansen as he brought the Cessna round for take-off. "No red carpet." He gave an almost relieved chuckle, then added, "Now we go home, eh?"

Gaunt nodded and fastened his seat-belt.

As they roared down the narrow airstrip and took off, he looked back for a moment at the tiny figures standing beside the Alfaburg huts. Then they shrank and vanished as the Cessna gained height and the cold wilderness became a grotesque dark patchwork far below.

It was raining when they landed at Reykjavik. The other Cessna was parked at the entrance to the Arkival Air hangar and Hansen taxied close beside it before he switched off.

"Thanks for the ride," said Gaunt as the engines died away. "Any idea when the next Alfaburg flight is scheduled?"

"Tomorrow maybe." Hansen unlatched the door on his side. "But with luck I won't draw it, *Herra* Gaunt. They are not my favourite people." He glanced at his wristwatch. "Like I told you, I have a date tonight. But I was thinking. If you're on your own, maybe my girl could find a friend—" He paused, then chuckled as Gaunt shook his head. "Your own arrangements, eh? Good luck with them."

Hansen left first, scampering through the rain into the shelter of the hangar. Gaunt followed at a slightly slower pace, his back stiff in its old familiar way, and made straight for the Arkival office. Anna Jorgensdottir was there on her own and her big cheerful face lit up as he entered.

"Lief is in town," she explained. "He went to see our lawyer, and a bank—but he telephoned. It looks like we can make the deal. Ah . . . you had a good flight?"

"No problems, cargo delivered," nodded Gaunt. He perched on the desk beside her. "Anna, what was in these crates?"

"The usual, I think." She searched her desk, found a slip of paper, and nodded. "Provisions, some equipment— nothing special. All we worry about is the weight, and if we've room enough."

He took the list, glanced at it, and laid it down again. The items looked like the kind of shopping list any isolated camp might need.

"You never check?"

"Check?" She looked bewildered. "No—why?"

"I just wondered. Forget it." He shook his head. "When will Lief be back?"

"He won't—he said he'd meet me at home." Stooping, she opened a drawer of the desk. "But he left me something for you." Reaching in, she brought out a small cardboard shoe box, the lid tied on with string. "You asked him about Jamie's things. We kept these—a few old photographs, some papers, personal things. Lief said you should take them, that a friend or a relative somewhere might want them."

"Someone might." He took the box from her and got on his feet again. But he had still another question in mind. "There's one thing I don't understand about the Alfaburg camp. Why do they keep their two groups of people so tightly apart?"

"*Nei*, I don't know—I've never been there," she admitted. "Ask Lief. Better still, if you're here tomorrow either Harald Nordur or Gunnar Bjargson should be around."

"Another flight?"

She nodded.

Gaunt thanked her and left, carrying the shoe box. Leaving the office, he made a dive through the rain and across the open to where the Matra was parked and tumbled thankfully into its shelter. Putting the box on the passenger seat, he started the station wagon, switched on the lights, then set it moving with the screenwipers lapping busily.

The airport perimeter road was deserted. He reached the gate, slowed, swung out, then took the main road towards the Loftleider Hotel. Lights glinted in his rear view mirror and he glanced at it briefly, seeing two cars coming up fast from behind.

A moment later the first car, a Ford, accelerated past him. Then, as it swung in again, it seemed to skid. Brake lights flared, the Ford swung almost broadside, and it came to a halt in a way that made Gaunt stand on his own brakes and pull up with a scream of tyre rubber. Behind him, he heard the other following car do the same, then an angry blare of a horn.

The car ahead had stalled. He heard the starter motor rasp unsuccessfully, heard the horn behind him blare again, and glanced back. There wasn't room enough to reverse clear and anyway the driver behind him was scrambling out, stalking forward in a purposeful way.

Gaunt grinned, deciding to let Icelander sort out Icelander. Then, suddenly, he realised the man from behind was at his door. It was yanked open and he found himself staring at the muzzle of a snub-nosed revolver. Above it, the man wore a stocking mask.

"Out," came the command.

Helpless to do anything else, he obeyed while a truck lumbered past on the outside, its driver unaware anything was wrong beyond a minor traffic snarl-up.

"Face the car, *Herra* Gaunt," said the same harsh voice.

He did, getting a glimpse of the driver of the first car coming over. Then, above the patter of the rain, he heard the man behind him draw a deep breath, heard the swish of cloth, and pain slammed through his head as the revolver came down hard on his skull.

Knees buckling, he collapsed against the station wagon with the world a red, aching haze. Still conscious, momentarily incapable of doing anything, he felt himself thrust aside. Then one of the men gave a satisfied grunt and he heard them running. Car doors slammed, both engines started, and as he tried to get up off his knees again the Ford roared away.

The car behind him reversed clear, then started forward with a grating of gears. It accelerated past a moment later, showering him with spray, giving him a chance to register that it was a Volkswagen, but nothing more.

Wincing with pain, he leaned against the side of the Matra for another minute while the rain still soaked down. At last, making an effort, he got in and closed the door. Shakily, he found his cigarettes and lit one, though it became sodden in the process from his wet hands and clothes. The shoe box had gone. He drew on the cigarette for a moment or two until he gained enough energy to curse, start the Matra, and drive on.

The lobby of the Loftleider Hotel was busy as usual when he walked through a few minutes later. But no-one spared a glance for one more rain-soaked arrival and he collected his key and went up to his room.

Calling room-service, he had them send up a large whisky. By the time it arrived, he had taken off his coat and had examined his head in the bathroom mirror. There was an egg-shaped bruise and some slight bleeding, but his thick mop of hair had helped cushion the blow—and somehow he felt the man responsible hadn't been trying particularly hard.

Once the floor waitress had been and gone, Gaunt used most of the neat whisky to wash down two of his pain-killing tablets. What was left of the whisky made a stinging antiseptic to clean the cut in his scalp; then he stripped off his sodden clothes, towelled himself down, and pulled on a dry shirt and trousers.

Going over to the window, he looked out. The rain was

as heavy as ever. Most of the snow that had remained was already washed away and the snowman which had been below was now a collapsed mound. Tight-lipped, anger giving way to bitterness at the way he'd been tricked, he crossed over to the telephone, raised the hotel operator, and asked for a call to Scotland.

It took about a couple of minutes before the telephone rang back and he was connected to the Remembrancer's Office in Edinburgh. Though the time difference worked in his favour, it was still late—from the Edinburgh switchboard girl's impatient greeting he'd caught her just about ready to leave and it was the same when he was put through to Henry Falconer. The senior administrative assistant almost always left on time. His wife insisted on it.

"Keep it brief if you can," was Falconer's greeting. "All going well?"

"No," admitted Gaunt reluctantly. "I've got problems."

"On the Arkival sale?" Falconer reacted immediately. "Drop the price."

"That side's all right. They'll buy at twenty-eight thousand," said Gaunt.

"Pounds or dollars?"

"Pounds." Gaunt glared at the mouthpiece. "Henry, I wouldn't give a damn if it was trading stamps. Did you hold out on me?"

"About what?" It came over the line as genuine bewilderment, then Falconer snorted. "All right, admit it. You've been drinking."

"If I had, I'd have fewer problems," said Gaunt. "There is a smell around the Arkival set-up and maybe about

the way James Douglas died. And I don't mean bootlegging. What do you know about Douglas that wasn't on
the file?"

"Nothing," protested Falconer weakly. "I told you your
job. You've to make a sale and keep the lid on the way a
certain lady is involved."

"While you play 'Rule Britannia' on your tin whistle?"
asked Gaunt sarcastically. "Henry, in the last twenty-four
hours or so I've been getting the treatment out here.
Someone did a damned good job of trying to scare me.
One of the local gendarmes turned up after that and
asked awkward questions. Now I've just been mugged
and robbed by high-class pros. So I want some help."

"What kind?" Instant caution was injected into Falconer's voice. "The last thing we need is to involve our
Embassy or the Icelandic authorities."

"Then run another check on Douglas, his R.A.F. record,
anything else there is." Gaunt pursed his lips, thinking
fast. "And do me a favour. Use some of your gilt-edged
golfing friends. Ask them what they know about an adventure-training camp called Alfaburg. It's run by a
Harald Nordur. One of his customers is Commonwealth
Engineering."

"I'll try." Falconer hesitated. "Just remember your own
priorities. You've a return air ticket. The moment you can,
use it. Anything else?"

"No. I'll call you in the morning," said Gaunt. "But say
hello to a certain lady for me, will you?"

"Who?" asked Falconer sharply.

"Your wife," said Gaunt innocently. "Who else?"

"Not tonight," said Falconer. "This is Tuesday—we never speak on Tuesdays."

Grinning, Gaunt hung up. He had about an hour left before he was due to meet Chris Bennett and he used part of it lying on top of the bed, resting, listening to music on the radio. Then he washed and dressed, examined the lump on his head again, and finally left the room.

But an idea had been shaping in his mind, one that had its seed back at the Alfaburg camp. There were that day's English newspapers down in the hotel lobby and he bought a *Financial Times,* then took it over to an armchair.

His tin shares were still sliding, as if they would never stop. But Commonwealth Engineering had crept up a couple of points and there was an almost too casual mention of them in one of the company news chat columns, as if somebody, somewhere, had caught a first hint of things to come.

The trouble was they were pricey, almost beyond his reach even if he threw in what would be left from next month's pay cheque. He put down the newspaper, scowled in a way that moved an old lady from the next armchair without his noticing it, then rose deliberately, went over to the desk, and got a cable blank.

John Milton, his stockbroker in Edinburgh, had enough of a sense of humour to have chosen as a cable address Paradise Lost. Scribbling quickly, Gaunt hoped the same sense of humour was still operating. He frowned at the final message and decided it was right.

DUMP TIN. BUY FIVE HUNDRED COMM. ENGINEERS.
SWITCH FOR OPTION ON HIGH LEDGE IF UNSTICKS.

He handed it over, paid for night-rate, then went out to
his borrowed station wagon feeling a whole lot better.

The rain had stopped and the traffic was light on the
wet, heavily puddled streets. It took only ten minutes
driving to reach where Chris Bennett lived, a large, modern apartment block close to the Hringbraut road. She
was waiting just inside the street door as the station
wagon drew up.

Gaunt got out, opened the passenger door, then shaped
a silent whistle of admiration as she came towards him
under the street lights. She wore a dark ponyskin jacket
loose on her shoulders over a long, simply cut dress of
rose-coloured silk, the neckline slashed deep down into
the hollow between her breasts. Her long, copper-bronze
hair, soft and glinting, was tied back with a ribbon to
match the dress and her only jewellery was a slim gold
bracelet on her left wrist.

"You look good," he said softly, helping her in.

"Thank you." She smiled at him as he got back behind
the wheel. "Don't look so surprised. Long wool underwear
went out of fashion in this country years ago. That didn't
help the pneumonia rate, but—"

"But I'll vote for it," said Gaunt gratefully.

They had agreed she'd choose the restaurant. It was in
a side-street not far from the fish docks, off the normal
tourist beat, with an unimposing entrance and only a

score of tables in a softly lit, quietly sophisticated atmosphere, with a piano playing softly in one corner. It was busy and from first appearance Gaunt guessed he was the only foreigner present.

The head waiter had a beard and wore a uniform which wouldn't have disgraced an admiral. He guided them to a table in an alcove, they ordered drinks, and Gaunt took one glance at the menu, then passed it to Chris.

"You order, I'll watch," he said. "No shark meat—I'll take my chance on the rest."

Summoned over, the bearded admiral seemed to approve of the arrangement. Their meal began with *riklingur*, tiny strips of specially prepared, delicately tasty dried halibut. The wine that came with it was in a plain glass carafe, unlabelled, but Gaunt raised an eyebrow after his first cautious sip.

"You approve?" asked Chris, her quiet brown eyes twinkling.

"Yes." He sipped again and nodded. "All right, and I've more sense than to ask about it. Who makes their deliveries—Lief Ragnarson?"

"He comes here sometimes," she said. "That's why we'll get ten per cent off the bill."

The service was unhurried, the piano relaxing but unobtrusive. They talked, each gradually learning a little more about the other, without ever appearing serious or probing too far.

The meal helped too. For main course they had a fried, thinly sliced lamb dish with a sour whey sauce and crisp vegetables. Sweet was a soft cheese *skyr*, whipped to a cream and after that Gaunt was happy to settle for brandy and coffee.

The piano player was joined by an electric guitar and a bass. A postage-stamp space in the middle of the tables became a dance floor, and they stayed on.

The bill, when it came, was impressive even with the promised 10 per cent deduction. The bearded admiral saw them out to the door, then they stood on the pavement for a moment under a sky which had cleared of clouds and sparkled with stars.

"It's late," said Chris quietly.

He nodded, saying nothing.

"So"—she paused and gave him a small half-smile—"maybe you'd better take me home."

When they reached the apartment block he parked the station wagon outside and went in with her. An elevator took them up to the fifth floor, where she took a key from her purse, unlocked her door, switched on the lights, and led him in.

Gaunt glanced around while she took his coat and her fur jacket and tossed them on a chair. The apartment's living room was small but spotlessly clean with a compact dining area over by the window. Teak-framed chairs and an old leather couch faced a TV set, and a couple of sheepskin rugs were carefully spaced on the polished wood floor.

"A drink?" she asked over her shoulder.

"Please," he nodded. "Whisky—if you've got it."

"*Ja*, but it's a blend, not a malt," she warned, crossing to a glass-fronted cocktail cabinet. "Will that do?"

"As long as it says 'Distilled in Scotland.'" He followed her over. She brought out the bottle, struggled with the unbroken seal for a moment, then sighed and handed it to him. Smiling, he gave the bottle-cap the statutory half-twist, snapped it open, and handed it back.

"Thanks. I only bought the damned stuff this afternoon." She flushed a little. "Hell, I suppose I shouldn't have told you that. But anyway, it's legal—not bootleg."

He hardly heard her. His eyes were on a framed colour snapshot above the cabinet. It showed a little girl playing with a ball. She was about three, with coppery hair and a wide, happy smile.

"Her name is Inga." Chris spoke quietly, watching him.

"Yours?"

She nodded. "She stays with my parents. They've a farm near Akranes—I get there at weekends." A slightly wistful smile touched her lips. "A farm is a good place for a child to grow up."

"Better than most." Gaunt waited while she poured their drinks, adding a dash of water from a jug. He found he had to clear his throat. "Patty and I—well, we didn't have that problem. But what about—"

"Her father?" Calmly, she handed him his glass. "We met in London. I was the original eager student, over there to study accountancy. I married him instead and we came back to Iceland—he's an industrial chemist and having an Icelandic wife gave him all the edge he needed to land a top job here."

"Then?" Gaunt sipped his whisky, watching her over the edge of his glass.

"He met someone else, just about the time Inga was born. Eventually they took off together—it was quite a scandal by Reykjavik standards. She was a clergyman's daughter."

"How long ago was it?" he asked.

"Over two years. They're supposed to be in Sweden now, but nobody's sure." She raised her drink in a defiant toast. "It's over. Anyway, I want to ask you about something more important. Jonny, are you still interested in Jamie Douglas?"

Taken by surprise, he nodded.

"Wait." She walked away from him, the rose silk dress hugging her long, slim legs. Opening a door which gave a glimpse of a small, neat bedroom, she went in. Gaunt heard a drawer open and after a moment she came back holding something very small and wrapped in tissue in one hand.

"Jamie Douglas came here once or twice," she said slowly. "Just to have a drink, or talk—he was lonely at times. I—well, I told you about the night he died. But I missed out something. Two nights before that, he came here and gave me this."

Puzzled, Gaunt took the tiny package and opened it. Inside lay a small gold medallion with a fine gold chain. The chain was broken. The medallion was a perfect imprint of a fingerprint, clear in detail down to the last loop and whorl.

"Has anyone else seen this?" he asked.

"No." She stood very close to him, looking down at the medallion. "He—he said he wanted me to keep it for Inga, that he'd won it in a poker game and it wasn't any use to him." She bit her lip. "I tried to say no, but he just laughed at me. He said there weren't any strings attached, that he'd maybe buy a new chain for it the next time he got lucky."

Frowning, he examined the medallion again. It was smaller and thinner than an American silver dollar and the obverse was blank except for a tiny hallmark and a hard-to-read serial number. Here and there the soft gold showed a few light scratches and signs of wear.

"Why keep it a secret?" he asked, wrapping the tissue round it again.

"When he was found dead?" She moistened her lips. "It just didn't seem to matter at first. I told what I'd seen at the office but even Anna and Lief refused to really believe me. Afterwards, when I thought about it more—I don't know. Maybe I was frightened, maybe I'd had enough. I still bruise easily."

"I know the feeling," he said softly. "But someone is still damned interested in James Douglas. Can I keep this?"

She nodded and he put the medallion in his pocket. Then, gently, he brought his hand up and stroked her hair. She gave a slight shiver, then suddenly the warmth of her body was pressed against his own. Their lips met and a low, soft sound like a sigh came from deep in her throat.

It was a long time later, and they were close together on the old leather couch. The lights were dimmed, an old Fats Waller record had just hissed to an end on the turntable, and there wasn't much left in the whisky bottle.

The telephone began ringing. Mumbling a startled protest, Chris stirred sleepily and her hair brushed Gaunt's face as she bent across him and managed to reach the receiver. Gaunt glanced at his watch and could hardly believe it when he saw the hands said three A.M.

"*Ja?*" Chris answered lazily, smiling at him. Then, as she listened, her expression froze. She asked a question, murmured a reply, then put her hand over the mouthpiece and stared at Gaunt. "It's Lief—Lief Ragnarson. You'd better talk to him."

Elbowing up, Gaunt read enough in her eyes to feel his stomach tightening as he took the receiver.

"What is it?" he asked.

"Trouble," rasped Ragnarson's voice. "I tried to get you at your hotel first. Then—well, this was Anna's idea. I'm sorry, but I had to find you."

"Why?" Gaunt came totally alert as he caught the anxiety in the big man's voice. "What's going on?"

"*Nei,* tell me one thing first," insisted Ragnarson hoarsely. "Were you driving that damn station wagon tonight?"

"Yes."

"And you left it outside Chris's apartment?"

"Yes," snapped Gaunt. "Why?"

"Somebody borrowed it," said Ragnarson tersely. "The

police contacted Anna at home twenty minutes ago—by phone, thank God, and that's where they think I am right now. The station wagon was in a crash on the airport road. The boy driving it was killed—a joy-riding car maniac they've had trouble with before. He'd jumped the ignition wiring."

Gaunt bit his lip hard. "You said the airport road."

"The way you'd have travelled if you'd gone back to the Loftleider," said Ragnarson, as if reading his mind. "*Ja*, and here is the sick part. The police say it was forced off the road and crushed against a wall by a heavy truck which came at it head-on. The truck didn't stop, but they have a witness."

"How do things stand with the police?" asked Gaunt.

"They're looking for a drunk truck-driver." Ragnarson gave a long sigh. "I—Jonathan, I don't know. I think something is happening I don't understand. That Matra was as distinctive as one of your damn British double-deck buses would be here. Suppose—"

"Supposing can wait," Gaunt cut him short. "What did Anna tell the police?"

"Just that she thought the station wagon was in the Arkival parking lot when we left tonight." Ragnarson paused awkwardly. "She . . . uh . . . she wanted to keep you clear of any trouble."

"Why?" asked Gaunt, his voice chilling. He looked round as Chris touched his arm, her expression worried and puzzled, but shook his head. "Tell the rest, Lief. What else is worrying you about tonight?"

"Nothing." Ragnarson's voice was hoarse again.

"Like hell," said Gaunt grimly. "Lief, I'm not the local law. You can be a happy bootlegger for the rest of your life for all I care, but ask yourself this—what really happened to Jamie Douglas?"

There was a long pause, so long he could almost hear Ragnarson thinking. Beside him, Chris had lit a cigarette. He drew on it once then put it between his lips. Her fingers weren't quite steady.

"Maybe you're right," said Ragnarson over the line.

"Then where are you?" demanded Gaunt. "I'm coming over."

"I . . ." Ragnarson hesitated briefly, then surrendered. "Get Chris to bring you. She knows where—and I'll tell you the rest when you get here."

The line went dead.

CHAPTER FIVE

Chris needed a couple of minutes to change into a heavy sweater and jeans, then they left. Her small blue Ford was in the apartment block's garage and she did the driving.

The city was empty and almost deserted; the only other traffic was an occasional police patrol car or late-night taxi. They took the main coast road north. Handling the car fast but carefully, she gave Gaunt an occasional sideways glance but said little, as if still numbed by Ragnarson's call.

Gaunt felt pretty much the same. He could have been in the Matra—could, in fact should if it hadn't been for the way things had turned out. But instead a boy was dead and he was travelling through the darkness to Lief Ragnarson's bootlegging base.

"How far?" he asked Chris.

"An hour—less, if things stay this way." She kept her gaze on the path. The headlights were lancing along the empty road ahead. "Get some sleep if you want, Jonny. I don't mind."

He reached over, laid a hand on her arm for a moment, then settled back and tried to doze. He had a feeling he should get some rest while he could, that chances might be few later on. The road snaked and curved, the shoreline often visible in the moonlight as they skirted round one long fjord then another. The signposts said AKRANES most of the way but just as he saw a glow which meant they were approaching the town they turned off on the Borganes road. Then, soon after that, Chris nudged him.

"Almost there." She nodded ahead at a small grouping of long, single-storey buildings.

Slowly, the Ford swung off the road and began bouncing along a rough track with the tyres spitting gravel. At the same moment as Gaunt realised the buildings were market garden greenhouses, Chris flashed her headlights. An answering flash came from the black bulk of a truck parked nearby.

Chris drew in, switched off lights and engine, and they got out. Two trucks and a couple of cars were already parked there, beside a small tumbledown brick building with a sagging corrugated iron roof. Taking his arm, Chris led him towards the building while the watcher who had signalled stayed in his truck and nodded a greeting.

"Friend of yours?" asked Gaunt.

"I know him," she admitted.

"Which makes you one of Lief's team?" he persisted.

"No. I just know what goes on." She paused at the door of the building. "Does it bother you?"

He shook his head. Pushing the door open, she led him

into a derelict pump-house festooned with pipes linked to a big, rusting central tank. Four men were working under the soft glow of a couple of big battery lamps, moving crates and small kegs, sorting them into a number of different heaps. They stopped and looked up for a moment, exchanged glances, then went back to work. Gaunt hadn't seen any of them before.

"Over here," said Ragnarson's voice. The big man stepped out of the shadows on the far side of the rusting tank and greeted Gaunt with a deliberate nod. When he spoke, his voice was curiously flat. "You made good time, Jonathan. You—well, you understand where you are?"

"I get the general idea," said Gaunt. "But when a thing doesn't concern me, I've no kind of memory at all."

"*Takk.*" Ragnarson's face showed relief in the dull light. He glanced at Chris. "No . . . ah . . . problems on the way?"

She shook her head. "One police car near the Akranes turn-off—nothing between there and Reykjavik. Any coffee around, Lief?"

"There's a flask in the corner." Ragnarson gestured vaguely and left her to find it, facing Gaunt again. "This building has been derelict since the market garden people built a new pump-house—the heating is by thermal springs, of course. They raise tomatoes, flowers, vegetables—like one or two others, they even try grapes and bananas. One of the staff is a friend of mine, so when we land a cargo of smuggled liquor this is the first stop ashore. But everything moves on, within twenty-four hours if we can."

He paused, barking a query at two of the other men who seemed to have finished their task. One grunted a reply. Taking a crate between them, the two men carried it out.

"And the trucks?" asked Gaunt.

"Two loads are away, these two will finish it," said Ragnarson. "If the police notice anything, market gardens often make early morning deliveries. If they stop a truck" —he smiled—"well, they will see vegetables. Another part of the arrangement, and they get delivered later." He paused. "That's not why you came, or why I telephoned. Am I right—did someone try to kill you tonight?"

"I'd bet money on it," said Gaunt. Chris came over and handed him a mug of lukewarm coffee. Sipping it, he added, "Don't ask me why. I don't know, except that someone seems to think I'm in Iceland to make trouble."

"*Ja.*" Ragnarson chewed his lip. "Jonathan, we made a landing on Monday night—this, and a whole lot more." One arm gestured at the diminishing liquor crates and casks now being carried out in a steady procession by his helpers. "Today I heard that the police and customs had been tipped off beforehand, except they didn't know how we land cargo. If that is true—"

"It's true." Gaunt almost smiled at the way Ragnarson's eyebrows rose. "A police inspector called Gudnason paid me a visit. He . . . ah . . . mentioned it."

"Gudnason." The big man breathed out heavily. "I know him, and that's enough. Did he say—" He stopped and shook his head grimly. "No, that can wait. The other thing matters more. Tonight, before I left home, Anna had a telephone call, a warning. Both of us were to keep our mouths shut about everything and anything concerning Jamie Douglas—or anything else that might happen. If we didn't"—he shrugged uneasily—"he said Anna would be a widow within twenty-four hours."

Chris touched Ragnarson's arm in sympathy. For Gaunt, the man's words again brought back the memory of the snowman outside his hotel, of the bottles smashing as an unseen marksman fired.

"What about the voice?" he asked.

"Muffled." Ragnarson shook his head.

"They threatened you, but what about Anna?" Chris's manner was tense. "Should you have left her alone?"

"I didn't," said Ragnarson. "Someone is with her. Girl, I'm not a fool." He paused. "No, maybe that's the last thing I should say to you, if I think back. Maybe I owe you an apology from then."

"About how Jamie died." Chris slowly shook her head. "I wouldn't blame you for thinking I was crazy. But now —" She turned to Gaunt, a pleading note in her voice. "Jonny, there are things you know about that we don't. Am I right?"

"Yes," said Gaunt warily. "But all of you might be safer if it stayed that way."

"Like hell!" Ragnarson made it an explosion. One massive fist grabbed Gaunt's coat lapel and tightened. "If someone starts threatening me, I want to know why."

"Here, right now?" asked Gaunt wearily, looking past him. Ragnarson's outburst had brought his loading squad to a halt. "I'd rather wait till you stop bellowing."

Ragnarson let go, signalled his man to get back to work, then smiled sheepishly after a moment.

"Sometimes I make too much noise," he admitted. "We're nearly finished loading. All right, why don't you and Chris come back with me? That way, Anna can hear too."

"There might be a watch on your house," said Chris.

"It's worth checking, but I doubt it," said Gaunt. "Anyway, Anna deserves to know." He turned to Ragnarson. "I had a phone call too, but on Monday night—and a small demonstration. But I can put a name to the voice."

"Who?" demanded Ragnarson, staring at him.

"Harald Nordur's sidekick, Bjargson." Gaunt almost smiled at Ragnarson's speechless disbelief. "I'm also ready to bet Nordur has someone in your office on his payroll, keeping tabs on you."

Ragnarson swore, a long string of incomprehensible Icelandic oaths spiced with some basic Anglo-Saxon.

"Now tell me something," said Gaunt as the tirade ended. "The coastguards had Muller's trawler on radar as she came in towards Snaefellanes. Then she swung out to sea again. Why?"

"Because my father and his father before him were fishermen—and smugglers as well." Ragnarson's rage subsided again. "I learned from them. If you know tides and currents and your coast, then you know that anything dropped overboard at a certain place will be washed up at another certain place." Putting an arm around Chris's shoulders, he said, "This one knows—her father and I grew up together. Muller released six liferafts filled with cargo—they were washed up on the beach twenty minutes later."

"You never lose any?" asked Gaunt.

"A life-raft load of whisky, once," admitted Ragnarson. He freed Chris and rubbed his chin. "We know who found it. Their entire village was drunk for a week."

The trucks left ten minutes later, grinding away into the darkness. They were followed by the rest of Ragnarson's men, who piled into one of the cars. Then Ragnarson shepherded Gaunt and Chris outside, carefully locked the old pump-house door behind him, and gave a nod to them both before he got aboard his old green Saab.

The drive back to Reykjavik was uneventful, the first of the early morning's traffic beginning to appear on the roads, the weather dry with a light wind coming off the sea. On the edge of the city Ragnarson pulled up at a telephone kiosk and Chris and Gaunt stopped a short distance back, knowing he was phoning home, checking that there were no problems about their arrival. Emerging, Ragnarson gave them a brief thumbs up sign then the two cars set off again.

They reached their destination a few minutes later. Lief Ragnarson and Anna Jorgensdottir lived in a converted farmhouse which sat on the fringe of a suburban housing development. A driveway led to the rear of the house and both cars crunched along its gravel and stopped at the back door.

Lights showed inside the farmhouse. When Ragnarson reached the back door it opened and Anna Jorgensdottir

was there to meet him. The couple embraced affection-
ately, then Anna beckoned Gaunt and Chris inside, into
the kitchen. Another figure smiled at them as they entered.

It was Hansen, the young Arkival Air pilot. He was
pulling on his coat and a double-barrelled shotgun lay on
the kitchen table.

"I thought you had a date with a girl," said Gaunt.

"*Ja.*" Hansen grinned. "But she's the understanding
type, so I cancelled. Anyway"—he winked at Anna—"I like
mature women."

Ragnarson slapped him on the back, then saw him out.
By the time Ragnarson returned, Anna Jorgensdottir had
removed the shotgun from the table and Chris was helping her set it with cups and crockery. Coffee was waiting
in a large brown pot and a bowl filled with warmed
Danish pastries went in the centre beside butter and jam.
Gesturing to Gaunt and Chris to sit down, Ragnarson
took his wife aside for a moment and talked to her
quietly. Then they came back and sat down at the table.

"Lief says you have a few things to tell us, Jonathan,"
said Anna. Her normally cheerful face was calm but serious and her hands were rock-steady as she poured coffee
for them all. "We're ready to listen, so—"

Gaunt nodded. He'd told some of it to Chris on the
journey back, almost using that as a rehearsal. Now, while
Ragnarson ate steadily, he began again. His start-point
was the way his hotel room had been raided, and he told
the rest that mattered briefly, including how he'd been
mugged and the shoe box stolen, the reception he'd en-

countered at Alfaburg and, finally, because Chris had agreed, he added the story of the gold fingerprint pendant.

As Gaunt finished, Ragnarson tilted far back on his chair and swore softly at the ceiling. Then he glanced at his wife.

"Anna?"

She was making an unhurried job of dissecting a pastry with her knife. Frowning, she finished before she looked up.

"If these people did try to kill you last night then by now they should know they failed," she said carefully.

Gaunt nodded.

"*Takk.*" She smiled almost sadly at Chris. "This pendant—I can understand why you stayed quiet. But may we see it?"

"Jonathan has it." Chris moistened her lips. "But if it matters, why did Jamie give it to me?"

"Maybe so he had it somewhere safe," said Gaunt. "Maybe he didn't know that it mattered till later on."

He brought the tissue-wrapped pendant from his pocket, parted the paper, and Ragnarson and Anna both frowned at it for a moment before shaking their heads. Neither had seen it before.

"I need time to understand all this," said Ragnarson. "You think you were robbed of that old shoe box and its rubbish because that damn Nordur hoped that pendant was inside it."

"The pendant, or something else," said Gaunt.

"*Ja.*" Ragnarson snapped finger and thumb together

aimlessly for a moment. "Apart from Anna and me, no-one knew about that box—till yesterday afternoon, when I left it with Anna for you."

"Pete Close, our mechanic, was there," said Anna. "So was Mattison, our other pilot—either of them could have heard."

"Make it three," said Chris quietly. "I was there too, remember?"

"You?" Ragnarson said incredulously. "We trust you like family."

"So we say two," agreed Gaunt. "Could either Close or Mattison have known about the liquor shipment?"

Ragnarson gave an embarrassed sigh and glanced sideways at his wife.

"Perhaps," said Anna dryly. "Sometimes Lief talks a little too much around the office. Then—well, there is the radio. If someone overheard us using it to talk to Muller on the *Orva*—" She paused, then shook her head. "Except it doesn't make sense. Jonathan, you blame Nordur and his man Bjargson. But Harald Nordur uses Arkival Air, needs us, so why cause trouble for us like that, whatever he maybe thought of you?"

"There doesn't have to be a connection," said Gaunt slowly. "Suppose he wanted to switch attention in the *Orva*'s direction, so he'd have a clear field to make a landing of his own somewhere else?"

"Because he guessed there was no way my people would be caught?" Ragnarson asked. "But what the hell would that damned Swede want to bring in?"

"Maybe some of the stuff you flew out to Alfaburg for him yesterday," said Gaunt.

The idea left the big man stunned and speechless. But Gaunt wasn't quite finished with him.

"You said Nordur wanted to name his pilot for the Alfaburg flights. Who did he want—Mattison?"

Lief Ragnarson nodded. "That's why I sent Hansen." He licked his lips. "I'd forgotten about it. So Mattison is our spy, right?"

"I wouldn't know. I've never even seen him," said Gaunt. "Just do me a favour. Don't charge in and slam him against a wall. Try and act normally, for now." He glanced at Anna for support. "I mean it. Make him behave."

"He will," she said. "I guarantee it."

Gaunt grinned. "Good. Last question. Alfaburg—what about those extra flights Nordur wants?"

"We've one at ten thirty this morning—Nordur's booked again as a passenger." Ragnarson scowled at the table. "Then tomorrow and the next day, one flight each afternoon going out empty and bring back passengers."

"Passengers?"

Ragnarson shrugged, disinterested. "Students. He's got this special course he runs now and again separate from the regular scheme. This one is being closed down early, for some reason, so we've eight students to bring out, two batches of four. It's the usual business. Fly them in to Reykjavik, bus them over to Keflavik, then they fly out from there International."

"To where?" Gaunt cursed under his breath as Ragnarson shook his head. Somehow, without being certain why, he had a feeling it mattered. "Can you find out?"

"Chris and I could," Anna volunteered. "We know some airline people."

"Do it quietly."

"And what about you?" asked Chris. "What will you do?"

"Right now?" He finished his coffee and glanced at his watch. It was nearly 6 A.M. "We could all use some sleep. Afterwards—maybe that depends on Nordur."

He left the house with Chris a few minutes later, after Ragnarson had yet again made sure there was no-one around outside. She drove her Ford in silence and Gaunt was too busy trying not to yawn to make an attempt at conversation. But as the car eventually drew in and stopped outside the Loftleider she faced him suspiciously.

"What are you really going to do?"

"A man I work for gets to his office at nine on the dot. I said I'd call him. Maybe I'll know then."

Leaning over, he kissed her firmly on the lips, got out of the car, and closed the door. She looked at him despairingly, then raised a hand in farewell and drove away into the darkness.

Inside the Loftleider the night desk clerk was tidying paperwork, getting ready to hand over to the day shift. Whatever he thought, he stayed politely impassive as Gaunt collected his key.

"Will you want a morning call, *Herra* Gaunt?" he asked.

"Two hours from now," said Gaunt. He winked at the man. "Nice city, Reykjavik."

Then he turned away and went up to his room.

It seemed more like two minutes later that the jangle of the alarm call dragged Gaunt back from sleep. He answered it somehow, forced himself out of bed, and spent a shive--ing couple of minutes letting the cold tap of the shower batter down on his naked body. But the needle-storm of ice-cold water left him wide awake and he ordered a pot of black coffee from room service once he had shaved and before he began dressing.

He was fastening his tie when there was a knock on the door. It opened, and as he looked round he gave a sigh. The maid who came in wasn't alone. Right behind her stood the burly figure of Inspector Gudnason and once again there were two coffee cups on the tray she was carrying.

"*Takk*." Gaunt nodded, as the maid put down the tray. Then, as she went out and the door closed, he faced Gudnason and said, "Coffee-break time?"

The policeman didn't smile. His blue-eyed, broken-nosed face was hard to read as, without waiting for an invitation, he poured coffee into both cups and handed one to Gaunt.

"I could have done this another way," he said quietly. "I could have had you brought down to my office. But I decided to back my own judgement, *Herra* Gaunt. Perhaps—yes, perhaps you might do the same."

They considered each other in silence for a moment,

two men similar in age and build, widely separate in background. Yet, somehow, Gaunt sensed he could trust the fair-haired man.

"Sit down," he said. "I'm almost glad you came."

"I hoped you might be." Gudnason settled in a chair as he spoke. "You know a boy was killed last night?"

"I heard." Gaunt stayed on his feet. "Lief Ragnarson told me."

"Then you also know the boy had stolen the Matra station wagon you were driving most of yesterday." The policeman's mouth tightened slightly. "His name was Nils, he had been in trouble, sometimes bad trouble, several times before—but he was only sixteen. Our people found the truck that hit him. It had been stolen too—and there was no trace of the driver, not even fingerprints on the steering wheel." He paused for breath. "Was it meant to be you in the Matra?"

"I think so." Gaunt chose his words carefully, trying to decide just how far he could go. "But I couldn't prove it, and it was nothing to do with Ragnarson."

Gudnason nodded, took a gulp of coffee, then set it down. "That boy's death was murder, *Herra* Gaunt. Despite what his wife says, I would guess Ragnarson wasn't at home last night. I can also guess why—but that doesn't matter." He built a slow, methodical steeple with his stubby fingertips. "At first, when I checked yesterday, the British Embassy didn't know you were in Iceland, *Herra* Gaunt. Later, they decided. I found that strange."

"They weren't told." Gaunt lit a cigarette. "When I came here, it was to settle up James Douglas's estate." He used the cigarette like a pointer. "I didn't know he'd probably been murdered."

"I see." It came from Gudnason's lips like a sigh. "*Fru* Bennett told us she thought he had a gun that night. We found a gun, yes—but it was back in his apartment, in a drawer. Suspicion is one thing, proof another, and we had nothing but her story."

"Suppose he was murdered," said Gaunt. "Suppose his killer was searching for something and couldn't find it. Suppose he searched the Arkival office, then took Douglas's keys and searched the apartment. He could have taken the gun with him and left it there—dead men carrying guns attract too much attention."

"And this 'something'?" Gudnason frowned. "Did it exist?"

"He made a good job of hiding it. Maybe he didn't even know it mattered so much." Gaunt took the fingerprint pendant from his pocket and swung it by the broken chain. "Ever seen one of these?"

Gudnason took the pendant, examined it carefully, then sucked his teeth for a moment. "I have heard of them, but they are not made in Iceland. The process involves a dental wax, the cost—" He stopped there, his eyes narrowing. "This number on the back could mean the makers have files, keep records."

"Then suppose you check it out," said Gaunt, grasping at the hope.

"I will." Gudnason put the pendant in his pocket. "Later, I may ask where it came from."

"And later I'll maybe tell you," said Gaunt. He stubbed

out his cigarette in an ashtray. "Look, there's not much more I know that makes sense—yet. But I think James Douglas blundered into real trouble, and perhaps I'm blundering the same road. Suppose I give you a name—does it go in a notebook?"

Gudnason made a deliberate job of patting his pockets and sighed.

"*Herra* Gaunt," he said, "I'm sorry. I forgot to bring one."

"Harald Nordur—he runs the Alfaburg camp." Gaunt saw Gudnason's surprise. "You know him?"

"Just heard of him," said the policeman. "He has a good reputation." He got to his feet. "Lief Ragnarson is coming to my office this morning, a formal statement about his station wagon, nothing more. But you and I will talk again, soon. And please, don't do anything foolish that might embarrass me. You understand?"

Gaunt nodded and saw him to the door. Then, alone again, he grimaced to himself. He could have dumped the lot in Gudnason's lap and got out—should have done that. Except that the original, crazy task which had brought him to Iceland had pushed him into a web which also involved Chris, Ragnarson and his wife and, he had to admit, his own stubborn temperament.

Five minutes later he placed a call to the Queen's and Lord Treasurer's Remembrancer's office in Edinburgh. When Henry Falconer's voice came on the line, it held the slightly sour note which usually meant Falconer was still opening the morning mail.

"Any luck with your friends?" asked Gaunt.

"I may have lost a few, chasing them the way I did," said Falconer peevishly. "As far as most are concerned, the Alfaburg training scheme does a good job—that's why they use it."

"What about dirt, Henry?" coaxed Gaunt. "You said 'most'—not 'all.'"

"An incident about a year back. Two fellows from an engineering firm strayed off-limits, or something. They came back claiming they'd been beaten up by their instructors but the confidential report from Alfaburg said they'd been drinking." Falconer paused. "The firm wasn't happy and stopped using the place."

"Nothing since?"

"Nothing," said Falconer. "And no-one knows anything about special courses—they're not listed in any prospectus."

"That doesn't surprise me too much," said Gaunt. "How about Nordur himself?"

"Very little. So little, it's surprising. Maybe he just doesn't like publicity. He has some kind of university lecturing background but if he ever got his fingers dirtied along the way it didn't reach any official file." Then he brightened. "I did better when it came to James Douglas's R.A.F. record. It was good in operational terms, including a commendation for gallantry. But he resigned his commission as an alternative to a court-martial—he was caught being naughty with squadron funds."

"The clever ones don't get caught, they're promoted," said Gaunt. Yet it was still a pointer. He wondered briefly if Douglas's ambitions might have stretched upward to blackmail, then put that aside. A totally unconnected thought entered his mind. "Do me a favour, Henry. Take a look at today's financial page and tell me how Commonwealth Engineering stand."

The line was clear enough for him to hear the senior administrative assistant's low-voiced cursing and the rustle of a morning paper. Then Falconer came back on the line.

"Two points up on the day," said Falconer. "I'm more interested in when we'll have you back here, doing some real work again. What's your situation?"

"I wish I knew, Henry," said Gaunt. "But have a happy day."

He hung up before Falconer could reply.

The call had given him more to think about, more loose strands which eventually must form some kind of final pattern. On an impulse, he checked the room's telephone directory and found a listing and address for Alfaburg's Reykjavik office. Tearing out the page, he tucked it in an inside pocket, pulled on his coat, and went out.

A yellow Volvo taxi had just unloaded passengers at the Loftleider's door. Gaunt got aboard, gave the driver the Alfaburg office address, then sat back while the taxi joined the traffic stream heading in through the morning darkness towards the city. The driver, a sad-faced middle-aged man wearing a thick wool shirt and a black fur hat, had his radio tuned to the American Forces station at Keflavik.

It was news-time. A senator had said something some-

where, there were floods in India and the usual chronic
rumblings in the Middle East. A Russian spy had been
arrested in London and two British businessmen had
been arrested in Moscow. The aircraft carrying the
United States delegate to the International Monetary
Fund meeting in Europe had touched down at Keflavick
and had spent the night there, because the delegate had
once served in Iceland as a G.I. Students had been on the
rampage in Japan. . . .

The driver flicked the broadcast off in mid-sentence.
They had reached the harbour area and were in the street
where the Alfaburg office was located. As the taxi slowed,
Gaunt saw Harald Nordur's grey coupe parked just
ahead. He let the taxi pull in opposite but stayed in it,
looking across the street at an old, stone-fronted warehouse block with a loading bay. A separate small entry to
one side had a brass plate at street level and a flight of in-
ternal stairs leading to where a couple of curtained windows were located on an upper floor. There were lights
behind the windows.

"*Takk*," said Gaunt, tapping his driver on the shoulder.
"That's it—take me to the airport now."

The man gave him an odd look but shrugged, switched
the radio on again, and set the Volvo moving. It was rock
music and a disc jockey all the way to the airport, and
Gaunt was glad to escape from it when he paid the taxi
off at the Arkival Air parking lot.

When he went into the office, Anna Jorgensdottir was
there on her own, sitting at her desk. Her elbows rested
on the desk, her chin was cupped in her hands, and she

was staring blankly at the map of Iceland on the opposite wall.

"Jonathan." She sat upright with a start and smiled, but her face showed a mixture of tiredness and strain. "Did you sleep?"

"Like the proverbial log." Gaunt glanced around. "On your own?"

"Lief is at Police Headquarters." Her voice was bright but forced. "They wanted to talk to him about the station wagon, but he should be back soon—so will Chris. She went to the bank for me, to draw some money."

"Want to talk about the rest of it, Anna?" asked Gaunt, looking at her. "Something has given you a scare. If it's something new, better tell me."

For a moment Anna Jorgensdottir seemed ready to launch an indignant denial. Then, instead, she silently opened a drawer of her desk and brought out a cardboard box. Her name and the Arkival Air address was printed in crude black letters on the lid.

"I haven't told Lief," she said, putting the box down.

Puzzled, Gaunt removed the lid. Then his eyes narrowed and he swore under his breath. A small doll dressed as a Viking princess lay inside, the kind of doll any tourist shop would stock. But the little princess, dressed in helmet and robes and carrying a spear, had her lips cruelly sewn together by wire staples.

"How did it come?" he asked, replacing the lid.

"By messenger, this morning—just a boy," she said quietly, putting the box back in her drawer. "He was gone before I opened it. I—well, I felt sick for a moment."

"I'm sorry, Anna," said Gaunt, and laid a hand on her shoulder. "I'm the one who started all this."

"Not deliberately. We know that." Abruptly, she changed the subject. "I spoke to my airline friends this morning. You're still interested in where Nordur's people are going?"

He nodded.

"Four have reservations to Luxembourg out of Keflavik tomorrow night, the other four fly to Brussels the following night." She rose as she spoke. "It's—well, unusual. None of them are going back where they came from."

"What about your own flight to Alfaburg this morning?" he asked.

"I'm going through to check on it now. She beckoned him to follow.

They went through to the Arkival hangar. Both Cessnas were parked under the lights. Pete Close was crouched under the starboard wing making some kind of check on the flap mechanism. A middle-aged man wearing flying overalls stood watching him.

"Mattison?" asked Gaunt softly.

"Ja, the one we talked about," murmured Anna, leading the way over. "He's flying this trip."

Mattison nodded a greeting as they arrived. He had a dull, heavy face, was built to match, and looked the type who could be unimaginatively competent. But he still had to be prime suspect within the Arkival team—unless the spy was Pete Close. Watching both men, Gaunt still noted and admired the way Anna Jorgensdottir gave no hint of her possible thoughts as she returned Mattison's greeting.

"Everything ready?" she asked.

"Cargo loaded and the weather report is okay, *Fru* Jorgensdottir," reported Mattison formally, ignoring Gaunt. "Pete is just being careful."

"Be glad I am," said Close, staying where he was. "Even your kind of fat backside would get frostbitten on a glacier." He glanced at Gaunt and his thin face twisted a grin of recognition. "How did you get on at Alfaburg camp yesterday?"

"Like I used the wrong kind of soap," said Gaunt.

Close laughed. "Out there, they don't use any."

Leaving Anna to talk to Mattison about the flight schedule and cargo list, Gaunt walked towards the opened main door of the hangar. Outside, multi-coloured lines of airport lights patterned the gradually greying darkness. He glanced at his watch, saw the time was approaching ten thirty, then noticed a car approaching. Moments later Lief Ragnarson's Saab drew in at the Arkival parking lot and stopped. Climbing out, Ragnarson spotted Gaunt and came straight over.

"How did you make out with the police?" asked Gaunt.

"Easier than I expected," said the big man. "Routine questions and a statement to sign, that's all." He thumbed towards the hangar. "How are things here?"

"Just waiting on Nordur—the aircraft's ready," Gaunt told him. "What's the cargo?"

"Groceries—and I checked," said Ragnarson. "They

came straight from the usual supplier, ready cartoned. But I sneaked a look inside a couple, just to be sure." He looked round and saw another car's lights approaching. "This will be Nordur now."

"Then play it like I told you," said Gaunt. "Be natural, whatever happens. As far as Nordur is concerned, you've no reason to think he's the one pressuring you."

"I'll try," promised Ragnarson. "But he can come looking for me. I'll be in the hangar."

"I'll tell him." Gaunt blocked Ragnarson's path as he turned to go. "Lief, have a talk with Anna after the flight leaves—just the two of you."

Ragnarson raised an eyebrow but nodded, and walked away. Gaunt stayed where he was while Harald Nordur's grey coupe purred in to stop beside Ragnarson's car. Then his interest quickened. Nordur wasn't alone. As the Alfaburg director emerged from behind the wheel the tall, thin figure of Bjargson climbed out from the passenger side.

They saw him standing under the hangar lights, hesitated momentarily, then came forward together.

"Still with us, *Herra* Gaunt?" There was sarcasm behind the words as Nordur greeted him. "By now, I thought you would have been on your way back home."

"Soon," said Gaunt. "Once I've taken care of what brought me here."

"Naturally." Nordur wore a heavy sweater under a dark, quilted anorak and serge trousers, the cuffs tucked into calf-length leather boots. He had one of the orange-coloured Alfaburg flight bags slung from his shoulder.

Coolly, he gestured at his companion. "Gunnar Bjargson, my Reykjavik manager."

Bjargson, who was dressed like Nordur and carried a similar flight bag, gave a grunt which could have meant anything.

"Tell them we've arrived, Gunnar," said Nordur casually. "I'll be along in a moment. And tell Ragnarson he'll have to squeeze you aboard."

Bjargson nodded and loped off towards the hangar.

"You're both going up-country?" asked Gaunt.

"Conference session, and one of the courses is ending," said Nordur. He contemplated Gaunt with an air that wasn't quite amusement. "I heard you went visiting. You should have let me know, and I could have arranged things better—my people dislike strangers. We aim at a complete cut-off from the outside as far as students are concerned. So if there's a next time—"

"It's unlikely," said Gaunt. "I've a reasonably full schedule."

"Your deal with Ragnarson." Nordur's eyes glittered through his spectacles. "Or is there more?" He didn't wait for an answer. Glancing at his watch, he gave Gaunt a brief smile. "Time to go. Alfaburg in daylight is quite picturesque from the air—a pity you won't see it."

As the man strode quickly away and disappeared into the hangar Gaunt grimaced to himself. Nordur had been playing with him, like a cat with a low IQ mouse. But Bjargson was flying with him. The tendril of an idea grew from that and he moved away from the parking lot, avoiding the hangar, going back into the office by the front door.

The office was deserted. Bringing out the page he'd torn from the hotel directory, he lifted a telephone and dialled the Alfaburg office number.

There was no reply.

He let the ringing tone continue for a few extra beats, then replaced the receiver. As he did, the office door swung open and Chris Bennett came in, unfastening her leather coat. Her face brightened as she saw him.

"Good-morning again," she said, giving him an almost shy smile. "I had a notion you might be here."

"Here, and just leaving," Gaunt told her. He saw her disappointment and grinned. "But I'll be back. Is your car outside?"

She nodded.

"How about loaning me it for a spell?"

"How long a spell?" She frowned, bringing the keys from her pocket. "Jonny, if you're stirring anything up—"

"At the British Embassy?" he asked innocently. "They only stir martinis over there. It depends how long I've got to wait."

Chris gave a relieved nod and gave him the keys.

"You're sure?" she asked again.

"Positive," he lied, and left her.

CHAPTER SIX

The day was slipping from darkness into a strengthening pre-dawn grey as Jonathan Gaunt unlocked Chris's car and got in. Then he sat and waited, the car lying close enough to the Arkival hangar to give him a clear view of the entrance. He heard the Cessna's engines start up, and a few moments later the little aircraft emerged from the hangar's shelter. As it slowly taxied past, heading for the runway, he could make out Mattison at the controls with Nordur in the co-pilot position and Bjargson peering out of the passenger window just behind them.

Gaunt kept watching while the Cessna took up position. Then it took off, climbing rapidly into the grey—and he started the car.

From the airport he drove straight to the harbour area and stopped a little way short of the Alfaburg office. He went the rest of the way on foot, got to the warehouse block just as a delivery truck pulled away from the loading bay, and could see no-one else around.

He reached the side entrance where the brass plate said ALFABURG, went in, climbed the concrete stairs, and reached an upper landing with a single door. It had a smaller version of the Alfaburg plate, with a bell-push beneath.

Whistling tunelessly under his breath Gaunt tried the bell-push and heard it ring on the other side.

There was no answer. Standing back, he gauged his distance, then swung his right leg in a kick, his heel hammering into the wood fractionally below the lock. The door shuddered and started to give and a second kick burst it open.

Gaunt waited a moment, conscious of the noise he'd made. But no sound came from inside the apartment and no one appeared on the stairway. Going into the apartment, he closed the door behind him and found himself in a hallway with doors leading off, the daylight from outside now strong enough to let him move around.

The apartment's basic layout came down to a small kitchen and bathroom, two bedrooms furnished in spartan style, and a large main room which was partly laid out as an office. An open cupboard door gave a glimpse of a photo-copying machine and a compact radio transmitter was located against one wall beside two metal filing cabinets. The cabinets were unlocked, so he ignored them for the moment and crossed to a desk which faced the window.

Some papers in a filing tray were mainly routine business letters, one of them an account from Arkival Air. He tried the desk drawers, found the top one locked, and used a heavy metal paper-knife on the desk-top to force it open. The tip of the blade snapped in the process, taking him by surprise, leaving him with a gash across one finger.

Sucking the cut, Gaunt made to toss the broken knife into a wastebasket. There was something already in it. Stooping, he lifted a newspaper and saw a considerable chunk of the front page had been torn out. It was that morning's issue.

Shrugging, he dropped the knife and newspaper in the bucket and turned to the desk drawer again. A cash box held a few kronur notes and an appointments diary lay beside it.

His fingers were on the diary when a floorboard squeaked behind him.

Gaunt spun round, then froze. There wasn't much else he could do. Pete Close stood just inside the doorway of the room, and the Luger pistol in his grip was pointed squarely and unwaveringly at Gaunt's middle. Close wasn't alone. Two other figures stood behind him, short, bulky men dressed in rough fishing clothes and similarly armed.

"Fouled it up this time, didn't you, friend?" The lanky English mechanic stepped nearer while his companions fanned out one on either side. "You walked right in, just like they reckoned."

"We all make mistakes," admitted Gaunt, raising his hands obediently as the Luger muzzle jerked an unmistakable order. "Nordur set me up?"

"It looks that way, doesn't it?" Close considered him derisively. "He left these two watching from down the street. Then I took a sick headache at work, left, and

practically followed you in. We just gave you enough
time to get settled."

"Then the rats came out of the skirting," said Gaunt.

His face stony, he didn't resist while one of the
strangers, who answered to Olaf, made a clumsy but thorough job of frisking his pockets. Then the other, called
Berg, produced a length of fine cord, jerked his arms
down again, and lashed his wrists tightly behind his back.

Harald Nordur had baited a simple, obvious trap and
he'd been fool enough to fall for it. Pete Close was the
only real surprise element—and even there he should have
guessed that Mattison was more likely to be in the clear.
The pilot was too placid to fit into any kind of intrigue.

"Real fishermen's knots, these." Tucking the gun away,
Close came over, inspected the job, then shook his head.
"Nordur really has it in for you, friend. Hard luck—there's
nothing personal in it with me."

"You're strictly hired help," said Gaunt. "Was it you or
these two who fouled things up last night?"

"Them. I—" Close stopped short and his horse-like face
showed a flicker of alarm. Then it was gone and he gave
an uneasy laugh. "I just give Nordur and his pal a little
friendly assistance for cash. Like now, when I've caught
them a burglar."

"How about Jamie Douglas?" asked Gaunt. "Where did
he go burgling?"

Close jerked as if stung and licked his lips.

"We've to keep you under wraps till Nordur gets back,"
he said. His eyes brightened and he nodded. "That's just

what we'll damned well do." He gestured to Olaf and Berg. "You two—come on."

Next moment Gaunt was propelled over to the cupboard in the corner. He was shoved inside, the door slammed shut, and he heard the lock click. Then one of the men outside laughed as they moved away.

Bleakly, Gaunt experimented with the cord binding his wrists. As Close had promised, his only achievement seemed to be that the cord bit tighter into his flesh. Leaning against the door, he turned his attention to his cramped prison.

It was well enough lit. A small glassed skylight too high above his head to matter any other way told him it was now daylight and blue sky outside. Down at his level the photo-copying machine took up most of the space and the walls of the cupboard were of uncompromising brick. Which left the door, which wasn't particularly solid. He could probably break it down with one good shoulder-charge, but that wasn't going to achieve much when the odds were either Olaf or Berg was parked outside with a gun.

Turning in the confined space, he bumped into the copying machine and looked at it again with a dull hope. The top casing was plastic but the trolley-style stand was metal and metal might mean a sharp edge, a way to free his wrists.

His back to the stand, Gaunt crouched down and began exploring with his fingers. But his luck was still out. Giving up, he sat back against the wall with a gathering sense of despair, then noticed an edge of paper protruding from the narrow gap opposite between the foot of the copying machine and the wall, newly dislodged from wherever it had been hidden.

Curious, ready to be distracted by anything, Gaunt wriggled round, felt for the paper, dragged it out, and pushed it in front of him. The smudged single sheet looked like a reject copy which had got lost. Suddenly, he became more interested, then was peering at the print, his own problems forgotten.

The sheet was headed "Operation Schedule, page six." Most of the space below, though it had printed badly, was a street map of a section of central Paris. Two Métro stations had been underlined and a star on the Rue de Rivoli was arrowed with "Hotel Meurice" written above it.

There was what might have been a timetable below, but it was unreadable.

Paris. Gaunt sat back, his mind racing. Nordur's "special course students" were leaving early, flying to either Brussels or Luxembourg, destinations only a few hours' drive from the French capital—if someone had good reasons for not wanting to go direct.

He thought of the story torn from the newspaper beside Nordur's desk, then of the news broadcast he'd heard. The International Monetary Fund's top men were heading for Paris, heading to a meeting brought forward because of current problems.

Gaunt closed his eyes and fought against the next part. But it made too much sense.

Eight men, drawn from God alone knew where, kept in isolation, put through training, given an operation schedule. The way he'd seen them scatter when that packing case had tumbled outside the Alfaburg bunker, the way men might react if they were handling—

Harald Nordur might be running a legitimate adventure training course for junior executives out there in the *obyggdir*, but his "special courses" were the ones that mattered.

This one had its target. Maybe each "special course" followed the same pattern.

And maybe he now knew the reason why Jamie Douglas had died.

Opening his eyes, Gaunt looked up at the little skylight window. The sun was streaming in; it would be early afternoon and dark again before Harald Nordur could return from a round-trip flight to Alfaburg. And a lot later than that before anyone, except maybe Chris, felt any particular concern at where a visiting civil servant named Gaunt had gone.

Sliding the slip of paper back out of sight and settling down into a more comfortable position, he resigned himself to waiting.

The time passed with an agonising slowness. Once every half hour or so the cupboard door was unlocked and opened, one of his guards looked in briefly while another stood ready in the background. Gradually, the little patch of sky he could see through the skylight began to dull.

Then, eventually, he heard a murmur of voices in the office and the cupboard door swung open again.

"Out," said Pete Close curtly, the Luger in one hand. He looked pale, almost agitated as he waited for Gaunt to obey, then bundled him out into the office, where the lights had been switched on and the curtains closed again.

Harald Nordur was standing beside his desk, the thug called Olaf hovering close by. As Gaunt was pushed nearer, Nordur came to meet him. The slim, bespectacled figure moved unhurriedly, his face wiped of expression. Then, totally without warning, he cuffed Gaunt hard across the face.

"Have a nice trip?" asked Gaunt bitterly, tasting blood in his mouth. He met Nordur's cold eyes unblinkingly. "It's a pity you made it back."

For a moment he thought Nordur was going to hit him again; then, instead, the man moved back a little. Taking out one of his slim cheroots, Nordur glanced at Close who quickly struck a match and lit it for him.

"I learned a little more about you at Alfaburg, *Herra* Gaunt," said Nordur. "One of the new intake mentioned he knew you. So—you were a British army officer, now you work for some government department." He paused, drawing on the cheroot, frowning. "I had already decided last night you were causing too much unnecessary trouble, that something permanent should be done about it. Now—unfortunately I can't spare the time to get the real truth about why you came to Iceland. Maybe you should be glad of that."

Gaunt shrugged. "You'd still end up with what you know already."

"Perhaps." Nordur sounded almost disinterested. "In that case, you were given a chance right at the beginning to keep out of what didn't concern you."

"The snowman." Gaunt tried to act and sound both angry and bewildered. "What the hell are you after anyway, Nordur? You want something Jamie Douglas had. You even killed for it, but you didn't get it—I can guess that much. But what is it, what's going on out at that camp of yours?"

Nordur looked at him for a long moment, then turned to the silent Olaf and signalled him out of the room.

"I was at Alfaburg when Douglas died," he said once the man had gone.

"Were you?" challenged Gaunt. "Arkival don't own all the aircraft in Iceland."

"True." Nordur gave a glimmer of a smile. "And there are other pilots, not to mention flying clubs, who hire out aircraft." He ignored Close's gasp of protest. "You are right, *Herra* Gaunt. Your countryman did have something of mine, something I had mislaid, and he found he also had—well, accidentally learned a little more than even you have. He thought he could put the situation to profit."

"Blackmail?"

"Exactly." Nordur drew on the cheroot again. "Blackmail by radio—because he thought I was in Alfaburg, because he underestimated. When he tried to use the radio that night, it was to get my answer. He . . . ah . . . got it."

Gaunt glanced at Close.

"Not me." Close quickly shook his head. "I gave him the office keys, that's all."

"So you broke the aerial before Douglas got there, were hiding in the office when he tried to use the transmitter. Pretty clever."

"Then one flick of a switch," said Nordur. "Afterwards, of course, we altered the setting—or Bjargson did. I hadn't thought of that." Suddenly, his manner hardened. "You could still make things easier for yourself, Gaunt. Douglas had a piece of gold jewellery that matters to me, a pendant. Do you know where it is, or who has it?"

Gaunt shook his head.

The man sighed, then glanced round as the office door opened and the other half of Close's back-up team came in.

"Okay, Berg?" asked Close anxiously.

The man nodded, turned, and went out again.

"That's it, then. His car's been moved. I—"

"You should have thought of it a long time ago," said Nordur coldly. "All right, you're not paid to think—you run errands." He eyed Gaunt. "The rest is a slight gamble, that you are on your own—or almost on your own. No outsiders too worried if they don't hear from you immediately. You might even be useful to us alive, for a little while."

Gaunt felt his stomach tighten, knowing what lay behind the words. But the telephone on Nordur's desk began ringing before he could reply.

Picking up the receiver, Nordur answered. He listened for a moment, then murmured thanks and good-bye. Gaunt barely noticed. His attention was on a tiny sliver of glinting steel lying on the floor close to Nordur's feet, the broken tip from the paper-knife he'd used to force the desk drawer.

"Bjargson says now," Nordur told Close, hanging up.

Close had gone as white as a sheet. But he nodded.

"Then get them in," said Nordur. "And put Gaunt back in his kennel."

Close shouted and the two men shouldered their way back into the office. As they did, moving towards him, Gaunt took his chance. As Berg reached him he made a pretence at a clumsy sidestep, let Olaf almost grab him, tangled with their legs in the process, then crashed on the floor and rolled.

Cursing, the two men swooped. Gaunt took a heavy kick in the ribs, then allowed himself to be hauled upright, apparently cowed. But behind his back his right hand now concealed the fragment of knife-tip.

"That was foolish," said Nordur, controlled anger in his voice. "Gaunt, one way and another you've caused me nothing but problems and your friends at Arkival have made them worse. I'm being forced to end something here, something that has been running smoothly for a long time." His mouth tightened, and he indicated Gaunt's captors. "You'll be kept alive, but these two have their orders. Give any trouble and you'll be shot through both kneecaps—which is as painful as it is crippling. You understand?"

Gaunt nodded.

"Good." Nordur's eyes still glittered like hard, polished stones behind his spectacles. "You'll be moved out of here tonight. I'll see you again, all going well, in a couple of days. I may have you killed then, I may not." He swung round on Close. "These two know you won't be back till tonight?"

"Yes," said Close.

"Then let's go," ordered Nordur. "Bjargson says he doesn't know how long we've got."

He led the way out of the office, Close following. As the outer door banged shut, Olaf and Berg tightened their grip on Gaunt's arms. He was hauled back towards the cupboard and thrown inside, falling hard against the copying machine. The door slammed and the key turned in the lock.

Darkness had returned outside, the little skylight above framed a patch of pale moonlight, and the interior of the cupboard was almost pitch-black. Gaunt eased himself down into a sitting position on the floor, ignoring the pain throbbing in his ribs and the other, familiar low-key ache starting in his back.

He had the broken knife-tip. Delicately easing the sliver of blunt steel round between finger and thumb, he began sawing at the cord binding his wrists. It was a slow job, needing time and concentration, and every now and again he dropped the sliver and had to find it again, groping blindly. But as he worked he spared part of his mind for Nordur, pondering what the Swede was doing, why the telephone call from Bjargson had been so important.

The cord was strong. It took almost an hour to saw through enough of the turns round his wrists for the bonds to come loose. Just as he finished the door was suddenly unlocked and thrown open. Gun in hand, Olaf looked in, and the door slammed shut again.

Quickly, Gaunt stripped away the rest of the cord, then massaged life back into his hands. The next stage . . . he had thought that out. It meant waiting till the next time the door was being opened and what came after that was a total gamble.

But it was that or nothing.

He waited, on his feet and ready in the darkness, mentally rehearsing what he had to do. An occasional murmur of a voice, low and muffled by the door, reached his ears. Minute crawled past after minute, then he heard muffled voices again. A floorboard creaked just outside the cupboard and the key clicked in the lock.

Gaunt hurled himself forward in a violent shoulder-charge. The door exploded outward, he heard a howl of pain as the wood crashed into solid flesh and bone, and he followed through in a long, skidding crouch. The man he had hit was staggering back, had dropped the revolver he'd been holding.

"*Nei!*" shouted an urgent, familiar voice as Gaunt grabbed the weapon and swung round ready to fire. "*Nei, Herra* Gaunt. It's all right—"

Gaunt stopped, swallowed incredulously, and lowered

the revolver. The man he'd hit with the door wore police
uniform. Two more policemen had Olaf pinned against a
wall, and Inspector Gudnason was grinning at him from
beside Nordur's desk.

"How the hell did you get here?" asked Gaunt with a
long heartfelt sigh of relief.

"Idle curiosity," said Gudnason dryly. He looked past
Gaunt at the injured policeman. The man's nose was
streaming blood as he glared at Gaunt, both arms clutching painfully at his chest. Gudnason grimaced. "Maybe
we should have knocked first, eh?"

"Sorry." Gaunt helped the man into a chair and left him
slumped there. He nodded towards Olaf. "This one has a
friend."

"Outside, in custody," said Gudnason. "He went out to
buy some beer. Do I get the feeling you wouldn't have
been included?"

"No way." Gaunt fumbled for his cigarettes and lit one
thankfully. In the background, the two policemen had
finished frisking Olaf and had him handcuffed. Drawing
on the cigarette, he told Gudnason, "One of that pair was
your truck-driver last night."

"*Takk fyrirr*," murmured Gudnason. He nodded to his
men, who took Olaf out, then walked over to the cupboard and peered in. "Temporary accommodation?"

"Till they moved me later." Gaunt leaned against the
desk, the reality of it all beginning to sink home. "How
did you know?"

"We didn't, at first." Gudnason frowned at his injured
officer, took out a large handkerchief, and shoved it into

the man's hand. "I was trying to find you, yes. Urgently. I had no luck at the Arkival office, no luck at your hotel— and your Embassy said they still haven't seen you. Then I began to worry."

"So you charged round here?"

"Thanks to *Fru* Bennett's car," said Gudnason. "Our traffic squad don't like long-term parking around here. One car crew checked the number of a Ford they noticed —then saw it being driven off by someone who certainly wasn't *Fru* Bennett. Unfortunately, they didn't mention it till they came off duty—but someone had the sense to let me know." He paused, then admitted, "The rest was guesswork. Just after we got here, we saw Berg coming out. We know him—and wherever he goes, Olaf is some- where near."

"What made me so important?" asked Gaunt.

"That I was looking for you?" Gudnason shrugged. "Among other things, to let you know I planned to visit this place with a search warrant. But your story first—it might save time."

"I came visiting too," said Gaunt. He saw Gudnason's expression and nodded. "Uninvited. But Nordur had set me up."

He sketched the rest quickly, his story punctuated by occasional sniffs and moans from the injured policeman who was now clutching a towel in place of Gudnason's blood-soaked handkerchief. Listening, Gudnason prowled the room in a state of tightly controlled tension.

"This map?" asked Gudnason as he finished.

"Still in the cupboard. The newspaper is in that

bucket." Gaunt rubbed a hand across his forehead. "Look, I know it's thin, wild—"

"It isn't, *Herra* Gaunt," said Gudnason. Reaching into his pocket, he took out something small which glittered in the light—the gold fingerprint pendant. "This is why I believe you."

"You traced it back?"

"To a New York custom jewellery firm," said Gudnason. "They made it eighteen months ago for a Miss Sarah Jones—the fingerprint was her own." He moistened his lips. "At the same time, I did something which I thought rather foolish—I ran a copy of the print through our own collection, and sent another copy by wire to Interpol."

"And you got lucky?" Gaunt stared at him.

"Interpol matched it," said Gudnason. "Sarah Jones was Sarah Haldoff, German-Swiss, wanted as a member of a Red Brigade terrorist team—until a year ago. She was killed in a botched attempt to hijack an El Al jet at Rome Airport."

Snuffling into the towel, the policeman staggered past them and out of the office. As the door swung, Gaunt caught a glimpse of other uniformed men waiting outside. Gudnason didn't travel understrength.

"You've still got to link her with Nordur," he said. "Prove it."

"We're trying." Gudnason looked around the room and swore under his breath. "Terrorists, this IMF meeting, God knows what all else. You damned English certainly stir things up without trying."

"I'm a Scot," Gaunt reminded him absently. "The poor damned English get blamed for enough."

"Scots are worse," said Gudnason. "They play lousy football and they even fish dirty. You've no idea where Nordur went to meet Bjargson?"

"No. Just that Close will be back tonight." Gaunt stopped short. "Maybe we should check with Ragnarson and his wife."

"*Ja.*" The same sudden doubt showed on Gudnason's rugged face. "My people can take care of this end—Anna Jorgensdottir is someone I like."

A police car with a sergeant at the wheel took them from the warehouse block, out of the harbour area, and straight into Reykjavik's early evening rush-hour traffic. Siren going, lights flashing, they carved a way out through the slow-moving lanes of vehicles spilling out towards the suburbs, Gudnason sitting silent and upright, Gaunt content to leave him that way.

They reached the airport shortly after 5 P.M., swung into the parking lot at the Arkival Air office, and found the place locked up and in darkness. Frowning, Gudnason nodded to his sergeant and the car swung out again, cutting across the outskirts of town, heading for Lief Ragnarson's home.

Gudnason cut the siren a full block away from their destination, then gave a grunt of satisfaction as they pulled up outside the house. There was a light burning in one of the front windows. With the sergeant at their heels, they walked up to the door and Gaunt rang the doorbell.

Nothing happened and, with a glance at Ragnarson, he rang again. This time they heard slow, shuffling footsteps and Lief Ragnarson opened the door. He looked out dully at them for a moment, then alarm flared in his eyes as he recognised Gudnason—and he stared at Gaunt as if seeing a ghost.

"Mind if we come in, Lief?" asked Gaunt, with a chilling sense of foreboding. "I think we'd better."

"I—" Ragnarson licked his lips, still staring at Gaunt, his voice hoarse and almost unrecognisable. "All right."

They followed him in, the sergeant closing the door, then staying in the background as Ragnarson led the way through to the kitchen. A half-empty bottle of *brennivin* sat on the table beside an almost empty glass.

"Ragnarson, I—" Gudnason hesitated and glanced at Gaunt for help.

"Lief, where's Anna?" asked Gaunt.

"Out." Ragnarson leaned his hands on the table, avoiding their gaze. Under the kitchen lights, his face was grey and had suddenly aged. "What do you want?"

"She's out where?" persisted Gaunt. He got no answer, and tried again. "Lief, I've told Gudnason what's been going on. We're here to help—and I saw that doll."

"*Ja.*" Ragnarson sank into an upright wooden chair beside the table, swallowed hard, then looked up at him as if struggling between faint hope and sheer disbelief. "Jonathan, they—they told me you were dead, to forget about you."

"They?"

"Harald Nordur, damn him." Ragnarson's fists clenched
knuckle-white as the words came slowly. "He's got Anna—
young Chris as well."

"Chris?" The fact hit Gaunt like an additional hammer-
blow. "You're sure?"

"I'm sure." Ragnarson took a slow, deep breath. "Nordur telephoned me at the office. He—he let me speak to
Anna. At least I heard her voice, just for a moment, then
she was pulled away." His voice came close to breaking.
"She was in tears, Jonathan—weeping. These animals—"

Silently, Gudnason moved round the table, lifted the
bottle of *brennivin,* filled Ragnarson's glass, and put it
into his hands.

"Drink it," he said. His rugged face grim, he waited
until Ragnarson had taken a long, deep swallow. "Do you
know where they are?"

"*Nei.*" Brokenly, Ragnarson shook his head. Then suddenly, he came to life again with a frantic urgency. "If
they saw you come here—"

"I doubt it," said Gudnason and glanced significantly at
Gaunt. "Even if they did—well, maybe that makes Anna
and the girl all the more important to them alive, as hos-
tages."

"But you can't guarantee it," said Ragnarson bitterly.

"I'm not such a fool," said Gudnason. He laid a hand on
the man's arm. "You have my word we try to get them
back unharmed. But I've got to know what happened,
what you were told to do."

"You've no choice, Lief," said Gaunt. He met Ragnarson's eyes and nodded. "I saw the Viking doll, I know what they're capable of doing. But I still say tell him."

In the background, Gudnason's sergeant had brought out a notebook and pencil. Quickly, fiercely, Gudnason shook his head and the man put them away again.

"Anna and Chris stayed till the Cessna brought Nordur back from Alfaburg," said Ragnarson slowly. "Then they left together—they took a taxi, because Chris said Jonathan had her car. They were going to Chris's apartment first, so she could pick up some clothes." His mouth tightened. "Chris was going to move in with us for a few days, because I thought it would be safer if Anna had company. Safer—"

"It made sense," said Gaunt. "Go on."

"An hour later, maybe a little more, I was alone in the office." Ragnarson paused and took another gulp from his glass. "That's when Nordur telephoned—and he let me hear Anna. Then"—he shook his head at the memory—"he sounded more like a devil than a man after that. He said I was to tell anyone who asked that Jonathan had decided to go off on a tourist trip north for a couple of days. That I was to make excuses for Anna and Chris, to pretend everything was normal—and that the Alfaburg flights had to go exactly as scheduled."

"And if you did all that?" prompted Gudnason.

"That he'd let them go," said Ragnarson. Laying down the glass, he spread his hands in despair. "I said yes. He told me to go home, for the night, and wait—that maybe he would call again, maybe not."

"*Takk*," said Gudnason. He talked quietly to his sergeant for a moment, then turned back to Gaunt. "He'll stay with Ragnarson and arrange some back-up to wait for us at *Fru* Bennett's apartment. Ready?"

"Wait," said Gaunt, his attention still on Ragnarson. "Lief, has Pete Close a pilot's licence?"

"For private flying, just single-engined stuff," said Ragnarson, bewildered. "He hires from one of the flying clubs."

Gudnason's eyes widened. He glanced at his sergeant and nodded.

"We'll check," he promised Gaunt, and left the rest unsaid.

It was another journey through the evening rush-hour traffic, the police car's siren wailing, Gudnason driving with a cold precision that wasted no time. Twice the messages coming over the radio began with their call-sign and the policeman answered. A net was being spread—whether it would catch anything was another matter.

There was no sign of any unusual activity outside Chris Bennett's apartment block when they arrived. But a plain clothes man was loitering in the doorway and two more were waiting in the lobby with the caretaker, a small, indignant man who handed over his pass-key with open displeasure and who liked it even less when he was sent back to his basement.

"Seen nothing, heard nothing," said Gudnason, as they took the elevator up to the fifth floor, one of his men with

them. "Most of the tenants are at work during the day."
He swore under his breath. "At work or prefer to be deaf
—it's always the same."

The elevator door opened and they walked the few
steps to the apartment in silence. Gaunt's fists tightened
as Gudnason used the pass-key and he barely noticed that
the plain clothes man had produced a revolver.

The door opened and he saw the apartment's lights
were on. He was first in, then stopped, in horrified disbelief.

A slim figure in a grey blouse and blue slacks was lying
face-down beside an overturned chair, head and shoulders on a blood-soaked sheepskin rug.

"Chris—" Brushing aside Gudnason's restraining arm,
Gaunt got to her and dropped down on his knees. For a
moment he felt paralysed, staring at the two bullet
wounds in her back. Then, lifting her gently, he cradled
her head in his lap and brushed her long fine hair away
from her face. Her eyes were closed, her skin was the
colour of parchment, but he sensed as much as saw that
she was still breathing.

"For God's sake get an ambulance," he appealed des-
perately to the two policemen. "She's alive."

The plain clothes man hurried to obey while Gudnason
dropped down beside Gaunt and felt at Chris's neck with
his fingertips.

"There's a pulse—a flutter," he pronounced in a low
grave voice, then sucked his lips. "I'm not a doctor, *Herra*
Gaunt. But I have seen people who were shot before.
Don't ask me what her chances are." Rising to his feet, he

drew a deep breath. "Stay with her. I have things to do, people to contact."

For a little while, time lost all meaning for Gaunt. Nursing Chris in his arms, he saw Gudnason leave, then return with some of his men, and was aware they were searching the apartment. He heard the wail of an ambulance siren, the squeal of tyres as it stopped outside, and then its crew were in the apartment carrying a stretcher, waiting while a white-coated doctor with a boyish, freckled face bent over Chris and made a swift, worried examination.

They took her from him, placing her gently on the stretcher, moving her out quickly. Gaunt went to follow them, but Gudnason stopped him.

"*Nei.*" There was sympathy in the policeman's face, but he shook his head. "You'll be in the way, that's all, and we have good surgeons. Give them their chance—there is something more important you can do."

"Like what?" asked Gaunt harshly.

"The man Close," said Gudnason. "He hired an aircraft this afternoon. When he took off he had three passengers —he picked them up at the far side of the airport, but one was a woman. He claimed he was taking some friends up the coast to Olafsvik." He shook his head. "Olafsvik airstrip say he didn't land there."

It took a moment to percolate, then Gaunt understood.

"He's due back?"

"About twenty minutes from now, from his hire times." Deliberately, Gudnason looked past Gaunt and pretended to consider the room again. "I think I know why *Fru* Bennett was shot. The only aircraft Close could hire was a Piper Cherokee, a four-seater—the girl would have been one too many, an embarrassment."

In terms of sickening, brutal logic it made sense and only strengthened Gaunt's frustrated anger.

"Close wouldn't pull the trigger," he said bitterly. "He'd hide under a stone first."

"That's what I hope," said Gudnason. "I want you there when we pick him up. Seeing you, he'll be more likely to talk."

"Suppose he isn't alone?"

"We still have to start somewhere," said Gudnason. He saw the lingering doubt in Gaunt's eyes as the sound of the ambulance siren began again outside. As it pulled away, he laid a hand on Gaunt's arm. "If there's any news from the hospital, you'll hear—and I'll have a car waiting."

The flying club operated from a small hut and a couple of old hangars in a corner of Reykjavik airport Gaunt hadn't seen before. When they got there, other police cars were already concealed behind the buildings, and armed policemen, some wearing mechanics' overalls, were waiting in the shadows. In the hut, one of the club's flying instructors had been on duty to book in the returning aircraft. Gudnason talked to him, then came back looking satisfied.

"Close is on his way," he said. "He radioed the control

tower a couple of minutes ago, and if he sticks to normal routine he'll park the plane here and sign off at the hut. But we'll make sure." He turned, gave a string of orders to his men, and watched carefully as they took up position. Then he touched Gaunt's arm. "The girl matters to you, I know. But—well, so does this."

It was a cool, moist night with a scatter of low, thin clouds obscuring the moonlight and, for once, the airport was quiet. An old Fokker freight plane lumbered in and touched down, then the runway lights were empty of life and they waited.

Gaunt saw the Cherokee first, a faint pinprick of navigation lights which appeared out of clouds to the northeast. A moment later the telephone in the hut rang and the control tower confirmed that their man was coming in.

Going with Gudnason, Gaunt watched from behind some empty oil drums while the aircraft made its approach and touched down smoothly. Swinging off the runway, it taxied straight towards them then stopped, the engine dying with a whine. As the propellor quivered to a halt the Cherokee's door opened and Gudnason pressed Gaunt lower.

Two men climbed out. One was Close, the other wore a heavy parka with the hood turned up, and they began walking together towards the flying club hut. Gudnason had a small metal whistle in one hand and let the men get well clear of the aircraft before he rose, putting the whistle to his lips.

The whistle shrilled. Three hand-held spotlamps flared on, pinning the men from the aircraft in their blinding white light.

"Police," bellowed Gudnason. "Stay where you are."

Close obeyed, throwing up one arm to shield his eyes. But his companion started to run, trying to escape the spotlamps, dragging out a gun from his parka while two of Gudnason's men, vague figures in the outer night, pounded to intercept him.

The man stopped and fired twice. One of his pursuers went down with a yelp of pain—and a single, staccato burst of fire rasped from a machine-pistol behind one of the spotlamps.

For a moment the man in the parka stiffened where he was. Then he pitched forward, fell in a sprawling heap, and was still. Outside the lights, the wounded policeman began limping back, helped by his companion.

Cursing under his breath, Gaunt at his side, Gudnason hurried over to the motionless figure. The man was dead. The machine-pistol's burst had taken him across the chest.

"A pity," said Gudnason with a trace of disgust, then frowned at the thin, bearded face. "Know him?"

"Franz Renotti, from the Alfaburg camp," said Gaunt, and shrugged. "He was chief instructor."

"Then they've a vacancy," said Gudnason. "But we still have Close."

They walked across the tarmac to where Pete Close stood visibly trembling, guarded by two policemen in overalls.

"Hello, Close," said Gaunt coldly.

The man stared at him, open-mouthed with fear.

"This is for Chris." Gaunt smashed a fist into Close's stomach, then almost regretted it as the man doubled up with a sob of pain and went down on his knees, cowering.

"Unfortunate, the way he ran into your fist like that," murmured Gudnason with a glance at his men, who stood totally blank-faced. "I think he'll talk all right—which is my department." He gave Gaunt a faint, encouraging smile. "No news is usually good news when a hospital is involved. That car is waiting—I'd go and find out."

CHAPTER SEVEN

Chris Bennett was still unconscious but her condition was rated as "slightly improved" when Gaunt arrived at the City Hospital. She was in the intensive care unit and X-ray examination showed one bullet had narrowly missed a lung and was lodged fairly harmlessly in the inner chest wall.

But the other had smashed a rib and was lodged against her heart.

Gaunt was with her when, around 8 P.M., the medical team decided they had to risk surgery. It was three hours later when they told him she had died from a massive, uncontrollable haemorrhage.

He asked if he could see her. A tall young staff nurse took him to the little room where she was lying, drew back the sheet which covered her face, then watched him anxiously.

For a long moment Gaunt looked at the pale, peaceful face. Someone had taken the trouble to tidy the long, copper-bronze hair. She might have been asleep; he wondered if it was just imagination that he could still see a trace of laughter in the corners of her mouth.

But there was a child named Inga in a farmhouse to the north who no longer would have week-end visits.

He thanked the staff nurse and went out of the room. Another nurse took him to an empty duty room, gave him coffee, then, wisely, left him alone.

Ten minutes later the door opened and he looked up from where he was sitting. It was Lief Ragnarson. The big man's broad face twisted a sad smile of greeting.

"Gudnason told me," he said. "I'm sorry, Jonathan. Anna and I—well, we both felt close to her too." Compassion and something else in his brown eyes, he added softly, "I can get pretty close to how you feel. And I know now why Anna was weeping."

Looking at the man, Gaunt struggled to the surface from his own feelings.

"I'm glad you came," he told Ragnarson.

"*Ja* . . . that's what I hoped. Gudnason say things are what he calls "stabilised" till morning. He doesn't want to see either of us till then." He considered Gaunt hopefully. "You look tired, the way I feel, and we have a spare room at the house. Tonight is—well, I could use some company. Maybe we both could."

Gaunt was glad to accept.

A police car was waiting outside the hospital and drove them out to Ragnarson's home. Once inside, Ragnarson produced a fresh bottle of *brennivin* and two glasses and they drank at the kitchen table, saying little, each with his own thoughts, each keeping it that way.

When the bottle was finished, Ragnarson showed Gaunt through to the spare bedroom. It was small and neat and smelled of pinewood, with floral pattern curtains and a matching duvet cover on the bed.

"Chris slept here a few times," said Ragnarson, staying in the doorway. "We liked it when she did." He drew a deep breath. "You only had a very little time together, Jonathan. But maybe that's still better than nothing."

The man went out, closing the door. Exhaustion flooding in on him, Gaunt undressed, got into bed, and put out the light.

But it was a long time before he got to sleep and the last thing that registered with him was that Lief Ragnarson was still moving around outside.

When he woke again, rain was pattering against the bedroom window and his wristwatch showed the time as 7:30 A.M. Noises were coming from the kitchen and when he found the bathroom there was shaving kit and a fresh towel laid out waiting on him.

After he'd used them and had dressed he went through to the kitchen. Lief Ragnarson looked as though he'd slept in his clothes, but he had made coffee and was frying bacon in a pan.

"How do you feel?" he asked Gaunt.

"Better." Gaunt poured himself some coffee and took the thick bacon sandwich Ragnarson handed him. He had command of himself again, though it took a continuing conscious effort, a deliberate shutting out of what had happened, of Chris in his arms, of her being wheeled away from that hospital bed, of the still shape he'd seen afterwards. "You?"

"Hopeful—it helps." Ragnarson frowned at the rain-streaked kitchen window and the darkness outside. "Gudnason telephoned. He's sending a car to take us over to Police Headquarters—it'll be here soon."

"That's all he said?"

"No. Things remain 'stabilised,' whatever the hell that means."

"We'll find out," said Gaunt.

"But will it get Anna back?" asked Ragnarson wearily. "That's what I want to know."

The police car arrived as they finished breakfast. The driver was Gudnason's sergeant. But they got nothing from him in the drive through the rain-soaked streets, and when they reached Police Headquarters they were kept waiting a couple of minutes before they were shown into an office where Gudnason and a stranger greeted them.

"Thank you both for coming," said Gudnason. He was another who looked as though he'd slept in his clothes, and he hadn't shaved. But there was genuine sympathy in his voice as he turned to Gaunt and added, "I had my own priorities last night—I'm sorry." Then, clearing his throat, he indicated the other man in the room. "Jacob Magnusson is here from the Prime Minister's office."

"What do we need him for?" asked Ragnarson rudely. He scowled at Magnusson, a tall, soberly-dressed man in his forties who had sharp eyes and a small, neat moustache. "Politicians—"

"Are sometimes necessary," said Magnusson, cutting

him short. He turned his attention to Gaunt, obviously expecting a more understanding reaction. "My Government sees the situation as one in which certain political guidelines may be required. That's why I'm here."

"That can wait," said Gudnason. "Let's sit down and get started."

There were chairs waiting around a large, glass-topped desk. Gudnason waited until the others had settled, then took his own place. He smiled slightly as he noticed Gaunt eyeing the furnishings.

"My boss's office," he said. "Borrowed—so don't spit on the carpet." He had a swivel chair, and tried it gingerly for effect. "First, what has been happening. The man Close is now co-operating fully with us on the understanding he will face reduced charges." He silenced Ragnarson's rumbling growl with a raised hand. "As a result, he has so far made two radio calls to Harald Nordur at the Alfaburg camp—scheduled calls expected by Nordur. One was late last night, the other about half an hour ago."

"Check calls." Ragnarson paled and licked his lips. "*Nei*, I never thought of that."

"My sergeant takes the credit—he got the details from Close," said Gudnason. "He also supervised both transmissions, meaning he kept a pistol stuck in Close's left ear." He suddenly remembered the government man with them and winced. "That's not orthodox, I know—"

"But effective," said Magnusson, unperturbed. "Go on."

"*Takk*." Gudnason brightened. "Close told Nordur everything was under control at the Reykjavik end. At the same time, we've made sure there's a complete news blackout on *Fru* Bennett's death and the shooting at the airport."

"How complete?" demanded Gaunt.

"Totally," said Gudnason. "The media people owe us favours, we're getting full co-operation. So even if Nordur is monitoring radio bulletins—" He shrugged and left it for something he considered more important. "Lief, your Anna is safe and well at Alfaburg—perhaps not particularly comfortable, but safe enough for the moment."

"You're sure?" Ragnarson swallowed hard. "You're . . . well, certain?"

"Close is. He says Nordur is gambling on her value as a hostage, the same way he still thinks he has Gaunt." The policeman considered his reflection in the glass table-top for a moment. "Close's instructions were to report for work as usual with you this morning, as if he didn't know anything had happened. Later, the man Renotti who was killed last night would telephone, and tell you to radio the Alfaburg camp—we've got the times. When you do, you'll hear Anna again, briefly. Nordur still needs your Arkival flights to get his men out of the *obyggdir* and started for Europe."

"And I suppose you plan on stopping me," said Ragnarson.

"No." The reply came from Magnusson, who looked shocked. "We advise . . . ah . . . apparent co-operation, for your wife's sake. Plan and schedule your flights as usual."

Ragnarson gave a relieved nod. But Gaunt noticed the way the man from the Prime Minister's office exchanged a glance with Gudnason, a glance which seemed to hold unspoken agreement.

"Keep everything apparently normal for now." Gudnason rose to his feet as he spoke. "Starting with going to your office now, as usual." He saw Ragnarson's doubt as the man got up. "Don't worry, you'll hear from me soon enough—that's a promise. My sergeant will give you a lift over towards the airport. But we'd like *Herra* Gaunt to stay for the moment."

Still doubtful, Ragnarson let himself be led over to the door. Once he'd gone, the policeman returned and sat down with a sigh.

"It's not so simple," he said, for Gaunt's benefit.

"I had that feeling," said Gaunt. "What didn't you tell him?"

"The same kind of arithmetic that meant they shot *Fru* Bennett," he said. "Nordur is totally shutting down, getting out. Counting himself, Bjargson and the three 'instructors' left at Alfaburg, he has thirteen men to get out of Alfaburg. One Arkival flight today, one tomorrow—that moves ten. Close is supposed to fly out and bring in the last three."

"But not Anna Jorgensdottir?" asked Gaunt.

Gudnason shook his head.

"They plan to kill her," he said. "She has seen too much." He tapped his fingers on the desk. "The same thing would have happened to you—after you were moved to an old fishing boat in the harbour. Olaf and Berg used the same boat on Monday night to rendezvous with an East German trawler and collect a delivery of weapons and plastic explosives, cash-and-carry style." He glanced apologetically at Magnusson. "They landed them later, while we were busy chasing our tails to the north, looking for Lief Ragnarson's liquor smugglers."

"Another small point may interest you," said Magnusson, using a forefinger to strike his thin moustache. "Sarah Jones—otherwise, Sarah Haldoff, the fingerprint on that pendant—immigration records show a Sarah Jones came to Iceland and left again after a three-week course at Alfaburg.

"When?"

"A few weeks before Sarah Haldoff was killed in the attempted airliner hijack at Rome," he said.

"If she gave that pendant to Nordur then something must have been going between them at Alfaburg," said Gudnason. "Isn't there a saying, 'like attracts like'?" He left it at that.

"Does it matter?" Magnusson's sharp eyes were fixed on Gaunt. "All it does is emphasise what we're up against. Even here in Iceland we've known there were rumors that several of the main European terrorist groups had set up a central training area somewhere—like an obscene variation of your Sandhurst officers' college in Britain." He paused. "Well, now we know. We have it here, in Iceland."

Gaunt nodded, wondering bitterly how many other terrorist operations had been born at Alfaburg, how many other fully trained and briefed teams had set out from there on missions of death and destruction.

"And this time it's Paris?" he asked.

"*Ja.*" It was Gudnason who answered. "That piece of paper you discovered named the Hotel Meurice. Interpol say three delegation chiefs to the International Monetary Fund meeting will be staying there."

All three sat silent for a moment, each with his own thoughts. The eight-man team from Alfaburg, armed, trained, fully briefed, could have brought off a snatch- or kill-type operation which would have caused chaos and upheaval.

But not now.

Yet what was left held its own problems, with Anna Jorgensdottir's life as part of the stakes.

"What happens next?" Gaunt asked.

"Like our masters, Gudnason and I started with different viewpoints. Now we are trying to reach a sensible compromise that might work." Magnusson gave a short, humourless laugh and glanced at the policeman. "One prospect was that we continued bluffing, that we let the Arkival flights bring out Nordur's men, then seized them." He shrugged. "I admit it would still have left Nordur and some of his people at the camp, with the woman as a hostage, but—"

"But it wouldn't work," said Gudnason. "Nordur isn't a fool. He'll want to be sure his first group get through safely before he risks the second group. We don't know what kind of all-clear signal he'll have set up."

"Something more than Pete Close's voice making happy noises on the radio," mused Gaunt, knowing Gudnason was right. He drew on his cigarette. "What was your way?"

AN INCIDENT IN ICELAND 151

"Nothing particularly clever," admitted Gudnason. "That we went straight in and sealed the place off. It wouldn't be easy, we knew that."

"Easy? The word is impossible," said Magnusson. "Overland, it would take a couple of days to get across the *obyggdir* to Alfaburg. The tracks will either be washed away or buried under snow. By air? If we flew our people in and tried to land on the Alfaburg airstrip the result could be a massacre."

"Helicopters?" suggested Gaunt. "They could land further off—"

"The *obyggdir* is silent, helicopters are not," said Magnusson, and shook his head. "What we need is some element of surprise, real surprise. The other factor is that our policemen are—well, just that. Nordur is sitting out there with a band of hand-picked, highly trained killers." He sighed and shifted in his chair. "Gudnason suggested one answer to that. I had to remind him that in Iceland we have political as well as practical difficulties in this situation."

"Political?" Gaunt raised a startled eyebrow. "Why?"

"We're a uniquely peaceful people, despite the fuss we make about our Viking heritage," said the politician patiently as if instructing a schoolboy. "We have no armed forces of our own—none, just a few coastguard gunboats to police our fishing grounds." He paused, tracing a finger on the desk-top. "The fact that we are members of the North Atlantic Treaty Organization is a constantly sensitive political area, and the same applies to the American military forces stationed here under that treaty."

"The Americans know what's going on," said Gud-nason. "They're willing to help. My idea was a plane-load of their paratroops—"

"They withdrew them last year," interrupted Magnus-son. "They would have to be flown in from the United States. But even if they were still in Iceland—no. Stub-born Icelandic pride, *Herra* Gaunt. Help and co-operation from other nations is one thing. But my Government is determined not to accept direct military assistance be-cause it would give a certain noisy political minority an ideal excuse to foment trouble."

Gudnason seemed to be waiting for Magnusson to go on. Yet Magnusson, suddenly, was in no hurry. It was as if he too was waiting, and Gaunt's mouth went dry at the thought of one possible answer.

"What's your alternative?" he asked slowly.

"It might be you," said Magnusson. "*Herra* Gaunt, be-cause of circumstances I made it my businsss to find out all I could about you. I have your Government's permis-sion to ask your help. I also spoke by telephone to a man named Falconer, who knows you well." He gave a slight, unexpected smile. "You have some unusual qualifications as a civil servant. You were a paratroop officer—and, of course, you've been at Alfaburg camp."

"You're asking me to make a drop on Alfaburg?" Gaunt felt an icy tension gathering in the pit of his stomach.

"Would you do it?" asked Magnusson.

He was there again, in the old nightmare, falling from the sky on the end of that partially opened chute, the half-formed scream buried in his throat. . . . Gaunt swallowed hard. There was another vision in his mind, the way Chris Bennett had been shot down, the sticky blood which had matted her coppery hair as he brushed it clear of her face.

"Yes," he said hoarsely.

"*Nei*." Magnusson shook his head. "But thank you." He smiled again, but with a new warmth and even Gudnason looked happier. "You were invalided out of the British army and I know why. What I have in mind is something different—maybe just as dangerous, but different."

"Well?" Gaunt felt the tension drain from his body and give way to an almost sick relief. "Damn you, let's hear it."

"The element of surprise." Magnusson got to his feet and paced the room for a moment. "Suppose there was another way to get you back into Alfaburg?"

"Like what?" asked Gaunt.

"The Arkival flight this afternoon." Magnusson made it a challenge. "It will land in darkness. There's a flare-path at Alfaburg?"

Gaunt nodded.

"The plane lands, goes to the far end of the flare-path, turns, and taxies back to the camp area," said Magnusson softly. "I want that Cessna to go in. I want it to fly five of Nordur's people out to Reykjavik—but if the pilot is willing to take the chance I want him to take two passengers in with him to Alfaburg. They'd get out of the aircraft when it was turning at the far end of the flare-path."

Frowning, Gaunt stubbed his cigarette and considered the idea, placing it against his memories of the Alfaburg landing strip. One man could certainly do it, two had a good chance—but in terms of time two would be the limit.

"Who's flying the Cessna?" he asked curtly. "And where will you find anyone fool enough to come in with me?"

"Mattison will be pilot." It was Gudnason who answered and he showed he understood Gaunt's surprise. "Mattison isn't bright but he doesn't scare easily. He's also the pilot Nordur will be expecting—and if you're thinking of Jarl Hansen, we need him for something else, phase two." He rubbed his chin. "And . . . ah . . . I'll be the fool coming with you, unless you've objections."

"I don't see any queue behind you," said Gaunt, and liked the way the big, raw-boned policeman grinned. "What's phase two?"

"Arkival's other Cessna," answered Magnusson. "Hansen will be flying it with a load of Gudnason's best men. Ten minutes, fifteen at most after Mattison takes off again from Alfaburg with his passengers—"

"Presuming he does," said Gudnason.

"*Ja.*" Magnusson suffered the interruption. "Hansen will wait for a signal from you, that you want him. He'll make an approach as if his aircraft is Mattison's Cessna returning with engine trouble, and he'll land. No signal means he stays away. You understand?"

Gaunt nodded.

"Good." The politician made a deliberate show of glancing at his watch. "I have to report back to the Prime Minister." He went to the door, opened it, hesitated, then looked back. "Let me be honest, *Herra* Gaunt. Even if this goes well, our official attitude must be that you played no part. But you'll have our gratitude."

He left. As the door closed, Gudnason winked across the desk at Gaunt.

"To hell with them all," he said cheerfully. Now we can get the real work done—and afterwards, you can show me the best way to fall out of aeroplanes."

"There's just one rule," said Gaunt. "You always make sure they're on the ground."

Over the next few hours a strangely assorted team of people each in turn played their part in the preparations for the move against Alfaburg.

Some, like the meteorologists, asked for detailed weather forecasts for the area, had no idea why. Others knew a little, guessed more, but said nothing.

At noon, a USAF photo-reconnaisance jet snarled down the main runway at Keflavik, took off, and climbed high into the sunlight.

Minutes later, a silver speck in the sky, it made a single high-level run over the Alfaburg camp with camera whir-ring. Swinging north, it continued its run along the east-ern edge of the Hofsjokull glacier and recorded a line of tiny, ant-like figures toiling across a snow-slope far below. Then, its purpose done, it returned to base.

In another hour a full set of photographs had been de-livered by helicopter to Reykjavik. At Police Head-quarters, a handcuffed, pale-faced Pete Close waited while Gaunt and Gudnason spread the enlarged aerial views of Alfaburg on a table.

"Good enough?" asked Gudnason.

Gaunt nodded. Every last detail of the camp was there in front of them, down to a speck which was a man walking across the open between two of the huts.

"Right. You"—Gudnason motioned Close nearer—"show us where they've got Anna Jorgensdottir."

Warily, keeping Gudnason between himself and Gaunt, the man pointed a trembling finger at a small hut close beside the bunker block.

"There—at least, that's where they had her last night." He licked his lips and glanced sideways at Gaunt. "Look, I never wanted anything to happen to her, or to the girl. You've got to believe that . . ." He saw only contempt on their faces and his voice died away.

They questioned him for several more minutes, piecing together more details about the camp layout. Then Gudnason signalled a waiting policeman and gave a sigh of relief as Close was marched out.

"Well, now I've an idea where I'm going," he said. "It helps."

Gaunt had turned to the other photographs, which showed the unsuspecting team of junior executive students toiling over the snow below Hofsjokull. He counted the tiny figures carefully and they totalled twelve—all ten students and the two "instructors."

"One less complication," commented Gudnason. "You . . . uh . . . know one of them, don't you?"

"Yes." Gaunt frowned at the dots, wondering which one was young Adam Lawton. Then he shrugged and pushed the photographs aside. Whatever happened, they'd be well clear of trouble.

"Time to move," said Gudnason, glancing at his watch. "I think Lief Ragnarson could use some moral support about now."

They reached the airport and the Arkival Air office ten minutes before Lief Ragnarson's scheduled radio-call to the Alfaburg camp. When they walked in, they found Ragnarson already had company—his two pilots, Mattison as stolid and unemotional as ever while Jarl Hansen paced around with all a younger man's eager energy. Both knew their roles, both had agreed without question.

The radio-call was to be at 2 P.M. As the minute hand crept round the wall clock Ragnarson switched on his transmitter, then made a clumsy, nervous fumble at the tuning dials. Murmuring an apology, Hansen eased forward and completed the job for him.

Then, his audience silent in the background, Ragnarson drew a deep breath and called the Alfaburg station. For a moment there was only a low hiss of static then Harald Nordur's voice grated from the receiver.

Their conversation was brief and in Icelandic. Listening, only able to guess what was going on, Gaunt saw Ragnarson's expression change suddenly. A moment later he knew why as Anna Jorgensdottir's voice came over the air. She said a bare half-dozen words, then Nordur took her place again while Ragnarson, his face white with strain, listened. He answered, Nordur signed off, and the call was over.

"No change." Gudnason made it a sight of relief. "Estimated time of arrival at Alfaburg is to be four P.M.—when it'll be good and dark. Everything said was nice and civilised, in case anyone happened to eavesdrop." He laid a hand on Ragnarson's shoulder. "You did well Lief—and Anna's still all right."

"*Ja.*" Ragnarson looked up slowly, his eyes fixed on Gaunt. "You know what she said, Jonathan? I was to look after myself till—"

"Till she got back," Gudnason finished for him. He kept his hand on Ragnarson's shoulder. "Our way, she will. Believe me."

He made it sound convincing, which was more than Gaunt could have done.

They had other visitors as departure time came nearer, more policemen—some Gudnason listened to with apparent respect, others who brought a suitcase containing the equipment Gaunt had ordered.

Finally, Magnusson arrived in a large black official Volvo. He came into the hangar where the two Cessnas were lying ready and his eyes widened.

Gaunt and Gudnason were dressed alike in white overalls, felt-soled ankle-length boots, and woollen balaclava helmets which covered everything except eyes and mouth. Each had a .38 revolver in a webbing holster and belt, balanced on the other side by a sheathed knife. Gaunt was quietly winding extra bands of tape round what remained of a double-barrelled shotgun, butt and barrels both sawn off until they hardly existed.

"You're ready, then." Magnusson sucked in a breath.

Gudnason nodded, picking up the small haversack which held their radio transmitter. Finishing the taping, Gaunt saw Magnusson frown at the bandolier of shotgun shells lying beside him.

"What load?" asked Magnusson.

"Buckshot."

Gudnason had suggested machine-pistols, but Gaunt had vetoed the idea. Getting out of an aircraft in a hurry was difficult enough without awkwardly lengthy burdens. But he'd fired a "whippet" shotgun before, courtesy of a Special Air Service corporal who worshipped them for close-range work—and a buckshot load, with its killing spread, made it a fearsome weapon.

"Good luck," said Magnusson awkwardly, and moved away.

A few minutes later Lief Ragnarson appeared with their pilot. Mattison climbed aboard his aircraft, the twin engines fired, and as the propellors began churning Ragnarson turned to face them. His lips moved, but his words were lost in the din as the Cessna's engines continued roaring.

Gudnason climbed in first. Following him, Gaunt closed the passenger door, then tapped Mattison on the shoulder. Nodding, Mattison opened the throttles and the Cessna began moving. As it left the hangar, Jarl Hansen gave them a wave from the other aircraft. His cargo of five heavily armed policemen were already aboard, pale blobs of aces behind the aircraft's windows.

Swaying and bumping out into the darkness, the small red and white Cessna reached the runway threshold.

Mattison opened the throttles, the bright lane of runway lights seemed to move towards them as the aircraft began accelerating, then they were airborne.

"You know something?" said Mattison in a surprised bellow. "I forgot to go to the men's room."

Gaunt swallowed, looked at Gudnason, and they exchanged a grin. Mattison had as dangerous a role as anybody, and it would be a lonely one. If his main worry remained his bladder they could have no complaint.

It was an uneventful flight, mostly through clouds, though a brief gap gave them a clear glimpse of the blue, moonlit bulk of the Langjokull glacier far below. An occasional lumping pitch by the Cessna emphasised that Mattison's handling was coarse compared with Jarl Hansen's skill, but neither Gaunt nor Gudnason were in a mood to complain.

The clouds stayed with them until they had crossed the Hofsjokull, then began to thin a little, but not too much for their purpose. Watching his instruments, Mattison at last glanced round.

"Almost there," he reported.

Gudnason nodded. "You know what to do."

Mattison used his radio, calling the Alfaburg transmitter. They answered and, winking at his passengers, he put the Cessna into a gradual descent. After a couple of minutes he used the radio again, waited for an acknowledgement, then began to ask for the airstrip flare-path. But halfway through Mattison deliberately closed the microphone switch in mid-word, removed his earphones, and produced a thin-bladed screwdriver. The Alfaburg voice had begun rasping urgently from the earphones, but he ignored it. Easing open a small inspection flap on the instrument panel, he peered closely at a set of exposed terminals, then carefully bridged the screwdriver blade across two of them. There was a sharp spark, a bang from somewhere in the rear of the aircraft, and the headphones went silent.

"Radio failure," said Mattison, calmly closing the inspection flap and putting the screwdriver away.

Anxiously, Gaunt peered ahead while the Cessna continued its descent. Then he gave a sigh of relief as the twin line of airstrip lights came to life on the ground. Harald Nordur had accepted the situation—and that meant the passengers on Mattison's return flight would be isolated from any communication once they took off.

Two minutes later the Cessna bumped down on the powdered white snow of the airstrip with Gaunt and Gudnason curled low in their seats below window level. Mattison let the aircraft complete as long a landing run as he dared, then gave a warning grunt and began his turn with the passenger door on the blind side to the camp.

Gaunt unclipped the door, threw it open, and went out in a fast, rolling dive. As he hit the crisp, hard surface he saw Gudnason follow him, a vague shape who landed heavily but also kept rolling. Then the passenger door slammed shut and the Cessna was lumbering away, taxiing for the huts, the wash of its propellors throwing up a fine, obscuring mist of powdered snow.

Gudnason had been badly winded. But, with Gaunt

half-dragging him, they got off the airstrip in a crouching run and flopped down in the cover of a low ridge of snow-streaked lava gravel and watched as the Cessna reached the camp and stopped.

Figures hurried towards it as the engines died. Gaunt heard Gudnason muttering under his breath as several long moments dragged past. Then they heard a shout and the camp's jeep drove out towards the aircraft. It stopped, and the glare of its headlights lit the scene as the figures began to transfer suitcases from the rear of the little vehicle into the Cessna's nose compartment.

"He got away with it," said Gudnason.

"Now it's our turn." Gaunt ignored the cold already seeping through his overalls and hugged the sawn-off shotgun to his chest. Their luck was holding, but their time was short, that maximum fifteen minutes from take-off. "Ready?"

Gudnason half-rose, tested his muscles, winced, but nodded.

They moved forward, white overalls blending into the hummocked surroundings of snow and frozen gravel. When they stopped, they were at the edge of the huts with a clear view of the aircraft. The last of the suitcases had been loaded, the nose compartment was closed again, and Mattison's passengers were climbing aboard.

There were five of them, apart from Mattison's unmistakable bulk. Gaunt moistened his lips. That left six men in all in the camp. He peered at the group who had remained at the jeep, counted four, identified one tall, thin figure as Bjargson, then another who might be Harald Nordur.

"There are two more of them around somewhere," he murmured in Gudnason's ear. "Keep your eyes open."

Moving further back from the airstrip, Gudnason at his heels, he led the way past the first of the dark, silent barrack huts, skirted a second one, then shrank back into a patch of shadow and frantically signalled Gudnason to do the same.

They were looking across at the concrete blockhouse. Light streamed from its open doorway, where a man with a carbine was lounging. As they watched, the man turned and another figure joined him. They heard a murmur of voices, then a low-pitched laugh.

"Well, we found them," said Gudnason in a whisper. "What about Anna?"

Gaunt pointed to the side of the blockhouse, to the small shed that stood there in isolation. It couldn't be seen from the blockhouse door, and he beckoned Gudnason to follow, then back-tracked, taking a new route through the silent camp. It brought them to the edge of the hut nearest to the little shed, with a stone's throw of open ground to cross.

At the same moment, the roar of the Cessna's engines starting up again reached their ears. They waited, and a minute later they saw it take off and begin climbing into the darkness, a darkness which became deeper as the airstrip lights went out.

"Now," suggested Gudnason impatiently.

"No." Gaunt made him wait. Soon what he'd expected happened—the jeep growled its way into sight from the airstrip, headlights sweeping the patch of ground they would have been crossing. The little vehicle stopped at the blockhouse door, its lights went out, and two men walked from it to join the pair who were waiting. They went inside together and the door slammed shut.

Seconds later, Gaunt and Gudnason were beside the shed. It had no windows, cinder-block walls, and a metal-faced door secured by a padlock. Gudnason drew his revolver, inserted the barrel in the padlock's hasp, and twisted hard. The cold metal of the hasp broke free and, giving a characteristic lop-sided grin, Gudnason eased the door open.

"Anna," called Gaunt softly.

Nothing stirred. Flicking a small pen-torch to life, Gudnason shone the narrow beam in a quick arc round the interior. It played on a row of kerosene drums, but nothing else. Swearing softly, he switched off again.

"Either Close was lying or—"

"Or they moved her." Gaunt suddenly knew where. "These two men at the blockhouse—"

"If she's there, we've lost," said Gudnason. "You'd need artillery to blast a way in."

"Probably." Gaunt sniffed the air, heavy with the reek of kerosene, then eased into the shed, tapping the nearest drums. Most sounded dull and full. "But maybe we could get them to come out."

"Eh?" Gudnason didn't understand at first, then gave a low chuckle. "A bonfire—why not?" Using the pen-torch, he found the cap on the nearest drum, opened it, used both hands to rock it, and listened happily to the splashing that came from inside. *"Ja,* I like it."

"Then it's your job," said Gaunt. "I want to check on Nordur."

He was on his way before Gudnason could argue, heading quickly through the camp until he reached the office hut. The door was closed but there was a light at the window and a thin trail of smoke rising from the chimney above.

Creeping to the window, Gaunt peered round the edge of the frame, then drew back quickly. Pressed against the cold outside wall, he found himself trembling in a way that had nothing to do with the temperature at the same time as his fingers tightened their grip on the cut-down shotgun.

They were both there—Harald Nordur sitting on a desk, an opened can of beer in one hand, a saturnine grin on his bespectacled face as he listened to Bjargson, who was talking as he opened another can. Also with them, completing the Alfaburg roll-call, the tall, sullen instructor nicknamed Garram the Gorilla was leaning against a wall near the stove with a rifle cradled in his arms.

Biting his lip hard, Gaunt fought against the temptation to kick that door open and send both charges of buckshot scything across the room.

That was all it would take, and Chris would be avenged. He let the idea go reluctantly, remembering Anna Jorgensdottir, remembering Gudnason working at the fuel shed.

He waited a moment longer while his senses steadied. Then, drawing a deep breath, he slipped away as silently as he'd come.

At the shed, he found Gudnason ready and waiting. Two of the kerosene drums lay tipped on their sides, gurgling out in a steady flow which was already flooding out of the door. The other drums were uncapped.

"Got a match?" asked Gudnason, holding up a kerosene-soaked rag which had been part of his overalls. "I don't smoke."

"Here." Gaunt handed over his cigarette lighter. "I'll be at the blockhouse, ready to go in. Light this lot, then try and join me. If you can't, play it by ear."

"I understand." Gudnason paused, looked past Gaunt and his eyes widened. "If the woman is in there, we're committed—we have to get her out."

Gaunt turned, then almost groaned. The kerosene flooding from the hut was flowing in a slow, steady stream following a slight down-hill slope that led towards the blockhouse. Once they set light to it and the other drums began bursting, the stream would be a blazing torrent—and the blockhouse would become an oven.

"It's too late to stop now," he said.

"*Ja.*" Gudnason managed what was meant to be a smile. "Well, at least if we get to signal that damn Jarl Hansen he won't need a flare-path to come in."

Leaving him, Gaunt hurried across to the blockhouse, reached the shelter of the parked jeep, waved back, then dropped down behind the vehicle.

A moment passed, then a tiny pinhead of flame from

the cigarette lighter became a blazing torch as the kerosene-soaked rag caught fire. He saw Gudnason throw the blazing rag, turn, and run—then with a noise like an angry drum-beat the whole fuel shed ignited into a yellow, searing fury.

Another blast sounded as one of the kerosene drums exploded. The blockhouse door swung open and a man stared out, his features bathed in yellow, flickering light as he shouted urgently over his shoulder. Then all four men were in the open, guns in their hands, standing as if hypnotised by the sight of the blazing shed and the pool of fire gradually flowing towards them. But only for an instant; then they were running, skirting the spreading pool, heading for the shed.

On his feet, Gaunt took two steps towards the open door of the blockhouse, then stopped short, shocked.

Gudnason hadn't tried to reach the blockhouse. Instead, he was at the edge of the flames to one side of the kerosene-fed inferno. As still another drum exploded, the policeman dropped down on one knee, took deliberate, two-handed aim with his revolver, and fired.

One of the four men dropped howling, clutching his leg. His companions spread out, their guns popping feebly against the background roar and crackle as Gudnason sprinted back from the glare.

"Damn you," snarled Gaunt despairingly, knowing the policeman was making a suicidal bid to win him time.

Turning, he ran into the blockhouse, down a corridor into a brightly lit central area, glanced round at the several doors leading off, and shouted Anna's name. If there was a reply, it was lost as another blast came from out-side.

"Anna," he bellowed again. "Where are you?"

"Here." It came muffled but distinct, from a door to his left. "Over here."

The door was locked and he kicked it open un-ceremoniously. Anna Jorgensdottir was sitting on the edge of a camp bed, wrists and ankles tied, sheer incredu-lity in her eyes as she saw him. Drawing his knife, Gaunt slashed through the ropes, pulled her upright, and shoved her towards the door.

"Move, Anna," he urged.

"What's happening?" she asked in a bewildered voice, staring round at the yellow glare visible through the room's high, narrow window-slit. "I thought—"

"Just move," he urged her. "We've got to get out, fast."

She obeyed, stumbling with him out of the room. Hus-tling the woman on down the corridor towards the exit door, Gaunt swore under his breath as she nearly fell.

"My legs, Jonathan," she said. "I can hardly feel them. These ropes—"

"It's all right." Putting an arm round her ample waist, he kept her moving.

He didn't completely see the figure that moved in the doorway ahead. But sheer instinct made him shove Anna down and dive after her as a rifle blasted and a shot whined over his head. Rolling over, gripping the sawn-off shotgun, Gaunt fired both barrels blindly.

The flat, twin blast brought a shrill, animal-like scream

of agony and the figure ahead fell as if jerked backward. Hauling Anna to her feet again, Gaunt steered her past the shattered body that lay in the doorway.

Gunnar Bjargson had caught most of the force of both loads at less than twenty feet and the heavy buckshot had nearly cut him in half. Gaunt heard Anna retch as she saw the result, but then they were out, in the open, and he was hustling her on again, away from the flames which now stretched like a river from the fuel shed to lap in fury against the blockhouse concrete.

A shot snarled out of the darkness and smashed into the wall of a nearby hut. Bewildered, uncertain where it had come from, he dragged Anna to the shadow of the hut, pushed her down into the snow, and hastily reloaded the shotgun as he crouched beside her.

"Here." He shoved the shotgun into her hands. "If you need to, just point and pull—one or both triggers."

"Me?" Her eyes widened.

"You saw what they did to Chris," he said savagely.

Anna Jorgensdottir's face changed in the wavering yellow glow that seemed to now bathe the whole of the Alfaburg camp.

"*Ja*," she said in a low whisper, taking the gun in her grasp. "I saw."

Gaunt had the .38. Something moved in the darkness and he fired, missed, and a reply snarled over his head. Moistening his lips, he peered into the yellow gloom, conscious of strange, approaching roar. Then he understood, grinned, swung round to tell Anna—and saw Harald Nordur stepping out from the far side of the hut, the flames reflecting on his spectacles and on the barrel of the carbine in his grip.

Anna screamed at the same instant as the carbine spat. Pain lanced through his head and he knew he was falling into a red, bottomless pit, while the world seemed to explode beside him and Anna screamed again.

When he came round, all he knew at first was that his head ached and a bright light seemed to be shining into his eyes. Slowly, muzzily, he realised he was in the Alfaburg office hut, lying on a blanket on the floor, the bright light a lamp that hung from the ceiling.

"About damn time you woke up," said a cheerful, familiar voice, and he blinked in disbelief as Gudnason bent over him.

The policeman looked tired. He had one arm in a sling. But the grin on his broken-nosed face was total and genuine. Putting his good arm round Gaunt's shoulders, he helped him sit up a little.

"You damn Scotsmen are hard to kill," said Gudnason, still grinning. "Jarl—"

Jarl Hansen knelt beside them, a tin cup in his hands. Gaunt took a swallow, tasted raw whisky, coughed as it burned down his throat, then let Hansen help him up and lower him into a chair.

There were several people in the office, a couple of them Gudnason's men, others strangers who wore civilian clothes but talked with American accents.

One, a tall man with crew-cut hair, cowboy boots, and a Texas patch on the shoulder of his parka, caught his glance and winked.

"What the hell's happened?" asked Gaunt weakly. Then a new thought struck him and he sat bolt upright, ignoring the fresh pain that stabbed through his skull. "Where's Anna?"

"On her way home by express helicopter—to Lief—she's fine," said Gudnason. His face sobered. "She saved your hide, Jonathan. When we found you, you were out cold, that bullet crease across your skull—and Harald Nordur lying with most of his head blown off almost within spitting distance." He nodded at Gaunt's unspoken question. "She killed him with that damned whippet gun. Then she reloaded and just waited."

But by then, Jarl Hansen had landed and Gudnason's police squad were going into action. Gradually, while the bustle continued around him Gaunt pieced together the rest.

Gudnason had drawn his pursuers away for a couple of minutes, taken a bullet in the shoulder in the process, then had managed to give them the slip in the darkness. He had used the radio, calling Hansen's Cessna in, the fierce blaze as good as any homing beacon.

But Hansen and his policemen hadn't been alone. Back in Reykjavik, Jacob Magnusson and his political masters had changed their minds or at least reached a compromise.

Soon after the Cessna landed, two large, unmarked helicopters had come churning in. The men aboard them wore civilian clothes but were U. S. Marines from Keflavik.

"And that was—well, that," said Gudnason, gesturing at the ordered bustle. "I've got one man slightly wounded, the Americans the same. So far, we've rounded up Garram and three of the others. That leaves one, but he won't get far in the *obyggdir*." He chuckled. "Mattison had no problems with his bunch. They landed at Reykjavik, marched off the Cessna, and most of them almost fainted when they saw the reception that was waiting."

"We were lucky," said Gaunt.

"Luckier than you know," said Gudnason. "They had explosives stored in that blockhouse, like you thought. The stuff overcooked in the flames—when it blew up, it took half the blockhouse with it. The rest—well, some of it was packed in the baggage-hold luggage, detonators inside toothpaste tubes, plastic explosive in shaving-cream containers. Enough to make a nice hole in the middle of Paris."

Hansen offered the tin cup again. This time Gaunt drained it, then gingerly ran a hand across his head.

"All you've got to do is part your hair a different way," said Gudnason. "*Ja*, and it could be an improvement."

He turned away to talk to one of his men. Gaunt sat back, letting his eyes close, head still aching, mind a confused whirl.

"*Herra* Gaunt." Hansen's voice made him look up. The

young pilot gave him a friendly nod. "I'm loading for Reykjavik, if you want to come now."

It was three days later before he left Iceland. Plenty had happened in that time, but he'd been divorced from most of it.

Taken in by helicopter, police had collected the two "instructors" from the student party beneath the Hofsjo-kull glacier. But the students, led by young Adam Lawton, had rebelled at the idea of being air-lifted out and were making a back-packing march of it towards civilisation.

The one man who had escaped from Alfaburg had also been found, stumbling around half-dead from exposure, and glad to be brought in. Now, like the rest of his companions, he was in custody at Reykjavik—but they wouldn't be there for long. As each of the terrorist squad was identified there were other nations with charges against them, and the Icelandic authorities were putting no obstacles in the way of extradition.

"Politics," had been Gudnason's dry comment as he saw Gaunt off at Keflavik. "Hell, at least it'll save us some expense."

Gudnason's arm was still in its sling. The night before, he and Gaunt had shared a quiet dinner with Jacob Magnusson. Magnusson hadn't said much, but the food and the wine had been the best and when they parted his handshake had been firm.

The Ragnarsons said their good-byes at the Arkival

office. Anna Jorgensdottir kissed him, Lief Ragnarson
shook hands, then pushed a small package into his flight-
bag.

Only Gudnason went with him to Keflavik. They had a
drink together, then the policeman grinned, nodded, and
ambled off as Gaunt's flight was called. It was only then
that Gaunt realised he'd never know the man's first name.

It was noon when his flight landed at Glasgow, in the
middle of the lunch-hour. Gaunt arrived in Edinburgh,
took a taxi to George Street, and walked into the familiar
block which housed the offices of the Queen's and Lord
Treasurer's Remembrancer.

Henry Falconer was waiting for him, sitting behind his
desk, arms folded, a slight frown on his face.

"Returned to the fold?" he asked, then nodded at the
pile of cable flimsies on his desk. "We've got the story—
the Remembrancer is reasonably pleased, particularly as
there's no publicity." He pursed his lips. "Still, there's the
Arkival transaction. I don't suppose—"

Gaunt handed him a thin slip of paper, Lief Ragnarson's certified cheque for the purchase of James Douglas's
share in the air-taxi firm. The formal papers were being
air-mailed as soon as they were completed.

"Good." Falconer thawed, got up, and came round
from behind his desk. "This girl who died—"

"Her funeral was yesterday," said Gaunt.

He'd been there, in the background. He'd seen her parents, dressed in black, and a tiny, copper-haired child
who was still too young to know what it had been about.

"I think . . ." Falconer paused, eyed him wisely, and changed his mind. "Look, that damned stockbroker of yours wants you to call him. He says it's urgent. Then— well, how about lunch?"

"Thanks. Another time, maybe." Gaunt left him, went out into the empty main office, and used a telephone.

John Milton was the kind of stockbroker who ate lunch at his desk. He reacted briskly when he heard Gaunt's voice.

"Who's a lucky devil for once, then?" he chortled over the line. "I did what you asked and Jonny my boy, you've made a killing!"

"The Commonwealth shares?" Gaunt hardly cared.

"Them?" Milton snorted derisively. "Sure, I got them— but I dumped them again, fast, no loss."

Gaunt didn't understand. "Why?"

"Why?" Milton sighed over the phone. "Because they began tumbling again. Commonwealth lost a packet on some Indian deal that went sour—but I switched you fast into High Ledge."

"High Ledge was a joke, like a window to jump from," said Gaunt. "What the hell are you talking about?"

"High Ledge are Australian mining shares," said Milton, almost spluttering. "They've gone up like a rocket in the past couple of days. If you sell now, you'll clear enough to pay off your damned car—maybe even make a dent in your overdraft."

"I see." Gaunt leaned against the desk beside him, thought for a moment, then said quietly, "Sell them.

There's something I'd like you to do with the profit—a favour."

"No problem," agreed Milton, puzzled.

"There's—well, someone I know in Iceland. A child—I'd like her to get it." He gave Milton the name and address and hung up.

Then he smiled slightly, his hand straying into his pocket. He took out Lief Ragnarson's parting gift and looked at it for a moment. It was a small block of crystal, beautifully engraved with a tiny map of Iceland. Underneath, in English, were two words: IN FRIENDSHIP.

He put the block back in his pocket, drew a deep breath, and marched back into Falconer's office.

"All right, Henry," he declared as the senior administrative assistant looked up. "I've changed my mind. Lunch—then you're going to hear about my expense account."